I0592851

# *The Yellow Butterfly*

## *& Other Stories*

Ashley Capes

For Brooke

The Yellow Butterfly

*Clank.*

Takashi slammed his hammer in time with the other men in the factory. Light from high windows gleamed on the steel sheet. Another ten just like it had to be finished by dark, else Shachō Nishimura would have two men—chosen at random—beaten and sent home without pay. His brutes wouldn't break arms or legs of course, since it wouldn't do to hurt productivity, but the bruises would be black enough.

And maybe it wouldn't matter soon.

The town of Baigan was teetering on collapse, or so it seemed. He'd tried to buy pears yesterday, and the merchants had only shaken their heads and sent Takashi back to the dust that climbed the wooden walls of the buildings around him. Shouts had risen from the harbour as he'd walked by but he hadn't turned. Another submersible accident – more of Nishimura's lust for gold gone to folly.

A shrill whistle sliced through the clash of steel-on-steel and hiss of steam.

Takashi stopped, wiping the sweat that stung his eyes. It ran down from his close-cropped hair; like every sane man in the factory, he kept it short. Less to get caught in one of the hulking, snapping machines – their mouths were ever-hungry. There was always someone shovelling piles of coal into the beasts' red bellies and their sparks were like tiny orange demons, darting everywhere.

It was different in Geinmo, supposedly, where electricity powered some of the machines. Takashi sighed; a new world loomed.

Foreman Ito entered through the gate. His face was red and his arms flapped in his black kimono as he strode along the rows of sweating men. "Shachō Nishimura is on his way. I want you working, do you understand? Don't make me regret hiring you." He shook his head, then hollered. "Two more submersible interiors due by the end of the month. That's ten days. Ten days!"

Hiro set his hammer down and leant close, grinning. "He seems especially shrill today."

"That he does, my friend," Takashi said. "Maybe he can no longer afford fruit either."

"No. I saw his wife returning from the market in Geinmo; they still manage to find good food."

An engine rumbled outside, followed by the now familiar hiss of a steam-wheel coming to a halt. Ito ran to the box-like office near the open entrance and jerked on the chain beside it. A dragon-shaped whistle screamed, and then it was back to work.

*Clank. Clank.* Pause, breathe. *Clank. Clank.* Pause, breathe.

Takashi swung his hammer in time with Hiro and the others, glancing at the entry as he did. Nishimura eventually entered the room, clothed head-to-toe in western garments: a suit with jacket, pants, shiny black boots and a ridiculous domed-hat concealing his silver hair. What did they call it? A bowler. Whatever that meant.

Fool.

But then nearly all the ex-Samurai were. They'd scrambled to find some way of maintaining power for years now. And for many, that meant business. Flying machines, submersibles, steam-wheels for land and rail, and even the new, motorised weapons. For others it was straight to the army. Where Father said he ought to have gone. *It is the duty of the strong to protect the weak.*

Nishimura spoke to Ito as he strolled down the line. The factory-owner's eyes swept across the floor but didn't truly appear to see any of it, as if his mind were elsewhere.

"... and you have not experienced any such problems?"

"No. No infestations of ants, Shachō," Ito said, a look of confusion passing over his face. "I keep the factory clean of insects and vermin, in fact—"

Nishimura raised a hand. Ito stopped speaking. "No matter, Ito, truly. It was an idle question; you know how I loathe such insidious creatures. And you need not concern yourself with the state of the factory."

"Shachō Nishimura?"

"I am closing it. Baigan is finished; work is moving to Geinmo. It's bigger and there is more opportunity for growth. The future of trade is no longer in submersibles in any event: it is in flying machines and steam-wheels. The latest model can carry four passengers; we only need the roads to improve."

"This is unexpected, I mean, we haven't even had time ...."

The two moved beyond ear-shot, voices buried by the clash of steel. Takashi stopped. Closing the factory? What would happen to everyone? Maybe Baigan was dying but that didn't mean the old snake had to drive the nail into the coffin.

"What's wrong?" Hiro asked. The other men were still pounding their part of the steel. "Why are you stopping?"

"You didn't hear?"

"No."

Takashi gripped the handle of his hammer. "He's going to close it."

Hiro took him by the shoulder. "Speak louder."

"He's going to close the factory," Takashi said, raising his voice.

The other men in his row stopped. "Who?"

"Nishimura."

Movement at the entry caught his eye. A young woman ran into the factory, her yellow kimono flashing in the patch of light. Takashi lowered his hammer. The way she moved ... such joy. Her silky black hair had been cut to frame her face and her eyes sparkled. Even the butterflies patterned on her clothing seemed alive.

It appeared she smiled simply because she could run.

Chou. She bore the same demeanour whenever he happened to catch a glimpse of her in the market square. Kiku had been the same; the innocence of childhood.

"Father!" she called after Nishimura.

Hiro nudged him, and Takashi returned to his work. They soon finished, and he moved to the pile of flat sheets, lifting it with another man, and returning to set it in place over the frame. This, like all the others, they'd curve to form the inner-lining of the huge passenger submersibles that took people all over the world.

The latest design boasted a clear bottom for observing the sea floor; the glass several *shaku* thick. Or 'feet' as those engineers who had returned from the west now said. Not something he'd ever book passage within – even had he the money.

By the time the small group returned, Ito was nodding again as Nishimura explained which pieces of machinery would be sent to Geinmo by rail and which would be sold.

Nishimura's daughter walked alongside, her head down, hair hiding her face.

The butterflies on her kimono no longer seemed to dance.

Hiro nudged him again and he returned to work. "I'm going to ask Ito about the factory closing. It can't be true," he said.

Takashi only nodded. He counted syllables as he hit the steel; he still had no ending that satisfied him but the poem was taking shape.

> *thistles dancing –*
> *an autumn wind*
> *muffles the long road*

~~

Ito had been powerless.

The factory closed as the leaves fell across the pale hills behind Baigan, and the men began to leave, searching for work. A few to Geinmo, some north to the mountains, others east, where word had filtered down: the Emperor needed steel workers for his new project, a great moving stair that would climb Fuji-san. Hiro was going to try his luck.

"Come with me," Hiro said where they stood before the iron-covered harbour. A sea breeze ruffled their clothing and tugged at columns of rising smoke. "There will be work – a dozen of us are travelling together."

Takashi shook his head as he watched the great crane on the dock, its squat body puffing steam as it struggled to lift the insect-like shape of one of the newer, sleek submersibles. The sides were fitted with long, thin cannons for torpedoes. Men waved flags and shouted as they coordinated. "Thank you, Hiro, but I will remain here."

Hiro sighed. "Are you sure?"

"I am. This is where she would have wanted me to stay."

"You can't live your life this way forever, in a dream, waiting for a tomorrow that won't come."

The man was right, but Takashi only shrugged. "All my memories of them are here. If I leave, there will be nothing left."

"Take your memories with you."

He put a hand on Hiro's shoulder. "A new place means new memories; the old ones will be replaced. Here, I hold them a little longer. Go, go to the Emperor and build his stair. It will be marvellous; you'll be happier there."

Hiro's expression fell. "Take care then."

Not until his friend's footfalls had died away did he turn back to the buildings. How small and fragile the wooden walls appeared compared to the stone and iron of the harbour. Or the watchtower beside the hulking walls of Nishimura Manor where it glared down upon them all.

He started toward the market. With what little money he had left he would buy his own tools and maybe the blacksmith would take him on.

Takashi passed through the shadows between the two-storey buildings, the eaves of peaked rooves extending over the street. Birds chattered from the thatching overhead but their songs were soon drowned in the bustle below. A patchwork of people filled the market: reds and blues, pinks and greens of kimonos and robes, but also the more muted greys and browns of western dress, their voices calling for goods before the storefronts.

The clock-master had closed his shop, but a pair of children had set up a blanket before it, selling pieces of broken machinery: springs, cogs, nuts and bolts all slick with grease. Caps and valves—he even saw a copper coil of wire. Where had they found that? One of the wrecks in the water? He did not ask, did not let himself think upon sunken submersibles.

He slipped through the crowds. His broad shoulders made it easy enough; people moved aside, sometimes after a glance at his expression. Sometimes without looking. Yet he didn't mean to frighten anyone.

He purchased a new tool belt and an old rivet-gun, the pressure-metre covered in dust.

Next came food. The catch was poor. Fish continued to die in the dirty harbour, and the prices were so high that he moved to the grocer and asked for the usual rice and fruit. He snared the last of the peaches, which was a stroke of luck, and smiled when Kenji wrapped everything and placed it on the bench before him, the older man brushing away a few grains of salt as he did so.

"Two *ryō*, Takashi."

Takashi hesitated. "Two?" He'd calculated less for everything he needed and could only pay for the rice. Or only the fruit.

"Prices had to go up again."

"Then I cannot pay for both, I'm sorry, Kenji. Keep the fruit; tomorrow I will—"

"Let me," a woman's voice interrupted.

Nishimura's daughter stood beside him. She held out a

few smooth pieces of gold to Kenji, who accepted the *ryō* with a bow. "Lady Nishimura."

"You know I prefer 'Chou', Kenji."

An older woman stood behind Chou; she clicked her tongue. "And the young lady should not be troubling either of you."

"It's no trouble," Chou smiled. She set a jar upon the bench as she spoke. Ants covered the inside, moving in and out of the earthen shapes within. "Aren't they wonderful?" she asked when she noticed his gaze. "Look at how well they work together."

He nodded. Perhaps they were, in their own way. "Do you keep them?"

"Yes, I'm building them a home, only I need a bigger jar already."

The older woman sighed. "And we should continue that task now, My Lady."

Chou waved a hand. "Soon, Kama. You're one of the men from the factory, aren't you?" she asked Takashi. "I'm glad I could help you, especially now that Father is closing it down."

Takashi nodded. "I am, but I cannot accept, Lady Nishimura." He bowed.

"Don't be foolish." She smiled up at him. "Let me. In fact, tell your friends if they will meet at the harbour, by the wreck, tomorrow at dawn, I will help them too."

Chou's servant frowned but only pulled Chou away from the stall. The young lady's yellow and purple kimono was swallowed by the crowd. Takashi looked to Kenji. "How could a man such as Nishimura have a daughter like that?"

Kenji raised a steel tin and spun its handle. Cogs ground

within, and the lid flipped open. He slipped the coins inside. "He is not her father by blood, you know. Orphan. Took her in at the insistence of his late wife. Few talk of it anymore."

"I see." Perhaps that explained why the man didn't seem to care for her.

He drifted away from the market, visiting the Smith, who wasn't able to make any promises. "It all depends on who stays. Maybe you should look at Geinmo. Or further south?" And then Takashi found as many of the old workers as he could, urging them to meet Chou at the harbour come dawn. Few seemed to believe much would come of her offer. Some seemed as desolate as he—especially the older men— while others were packing their possessions.

And still he could not join them.

Instead, he headed for the glistening water. Better than sitting at home—the empty walls, the empty table, the flowerbed shrinking to grey.

His footsteps counted the syllables:

*thistles dancing –*
*an autumn wind*
*drowns out my heart*

~~

Before dawn he met several more men where they stood together in the grey light by one of the old submersibles. Rust ran from its huge rivets. Patina discoloured the body and grime ringed the portholes, obscuring the controls within: a forest of levers and gear shifts, none of which he'd ever truly understood.

Maybe it would be better never to see another made here.

Deadly machines. Not just for the navigators and passengers, but whole towns, like Baigan, where they had left only misery in the frothing wake of their waves. He greeted a few of the men and listened to their talk. There was little confidence in Chou but the same thing brought them here – desperation, perhaps, more than curiosity.

And she did come.

Before the sun broke free of the horizon Chou appeared, her servant in tow. The older woman carried a chest, her weary face tight with strain. She dropped it to the deck with a sigh. Muffled clinking followed, and the men exchanged glances.

Chou smiled at them. "Thank you for trusting Takashi; I am glad you have come to meet me. I know my father has made your lives difficult in closing the factory. In a small way, I hope to help." She paused to nod to her servant. "Kama has small piles of *ryō* wrapped in cloth. Each of you take one and let it help you on your way; for if you take gold you must leave Baigan. My father will not be pleased."

One of the men spoke. "And we can simply take them and owe you nothing?"

"Yes."

Takashi frowned. "Lady, if you have taken this from your father ...."

"Do not worry. By the time he discovers it missing it will be too late."

A voice spoke from the end of the pier. "Or very nearly too late."

Nishimura raised a lantern, turning a tiny lever to increase the brightness. It lit the dull faces of half a dozen men, all armed with long *tachi* and smaller knives. Two also carried modified matchlock rifles. A thin shaft jutted from above each weapon, a dial on the side. With it, each man could load and fire half a dozen rounds far quicker than usual. Another terror of the new world.

The gathered factory workers fell silent, and Chou let out a gasp.

Nishimura gestured for two of his men to take the chest; a third he directed to Chou, after a glance to Kama. The servant's wrinkled face did not change, but Chou spun on the older woman. "Why?"

Kama glanced away.

The third man took Chou by the arm, wrenching her around and dragging the young woman toward her father. She cried out, and Takashi took a step forward.

One of the riflemen raised his weapon.

Taskashi stopped.

"And now, gentlemen, I trust you will continue to seek employment elsewhere." Nishimura turned his glare upon his daughter, then cut the lantern light. He turned to leave, and their shadows receded along the boards, the figure of Chou struggling against them.

Takashi ground his teeth but did not follow.

They'd only shoot him—or worse, hurt Chou.

~~

Two days passed, and he ate the rest of his food and spent the last of his money. And not once did she appear in the market, nor did anyone in Baigan hear from her. Not Kenji or any of the other shopkeepers. Not even Ito, who

Takashi stopped as the man attempted to close his door on the second evening. "Takashi, listen to me: I don't know anything. I'm sure she's well." The man's jowls seemed to sink further toward his chin, and he could not meet Takashi's gaze.

"Ito, don't lie. You dined there last night at Nishimura's invitation; you must know something."

"I know he's offering to move me and my family to Geinmo."

Of course. "But you didn't see her?"

"No, Takashi. Now go home. And change your clothes for God's sake. You smell terrible." He slammed his door.

Takashi shook his head. Not at the comment about his clothing—it was true, he needed to change—but at the lie. Ito knew something. And of course the man was afraid to speak: his future depended upon staying on Nishimura's good side.

Takashi wove through the front garden with its red maples and turned down the lane beside the house, angling toward the square. He'd reached the edge when a creak echoed in the lane. A gate swung open, and a woman stepped out. Ito's wife.

She waved him closer, hands slipping from the sleeves of her blue kimono. She had tied her obi in some haste, as her sash sat a little crooked.

"Haru-san?"

"Quickly," she said. Her voice was hard to hear over the murmuring from the market and the roar of a steam-wheel passing somewhere nearby. "My husband was upset when he came home last night—I fear Nishimura has hurt Chou."

A chill spread across Takashi's body. "He what?"

"Yes. But do not ask any more, Takashi. A darkness hangs over him since his wife died."

He folded his arms. "Then you should not have told me."

"No, that is *why* I tell you. Your name was mentioned: Shachō doesn't like that you are asking after Chou. Make your peace with it, return to your life."

Takashi smiled. "I have had no peace for years." He thanked her and headed for the square.

"You cannot bring them back, Takashi, not this way, not any way," she called.

He offered no answer.

Instead, he returned home, lit his lamps and removed his clothes. He wiped himself down with a wet rag, stepped into a fresh kosode, then brushed at the sleeves of his haori before pulling the coat on too. Then he ran a razor across his jaw. A tiny spot of red bloomed in the mirror, and he wiped his cheek with the back of his hand.

Finally, he knelt by a screen then slid it aside.

And blinked.

Ants.

Ants had crawled within, finding a crack, a space between timber and earth: like smoke or water, somehow they'd found a way. And there they covered the floorboards before a steel chest.

Swarming in place.

They moved in a pattern, like a kanji painted by a rough hand. It seemed to spell out the word for 'tower.' He leant closer; there was no doubt. That was the word. And there was only one tower in Baigan, the tower beside the manor. The building looked across the ocean and collected signals from the flashing mirrors when the submersibles rose.

And so there he would go.

He lifted the lid of the chest and drew out a blue silken scarf. A boat with a single sail crossed the waves. This he took and tied around his forearm. "Shima ..." He could not finish. Would she approve? Yes. She had to. Next, he lifted a child's *hagoita*-paddle covered in cherry blossoms. Kiku would have urged him on. "You would have liked Chou," he told his daughter.

He hooked the paddle in his belt.

Finally, he lifted the new smith's hammer from where it leant against the doorframe and walked into the darkening night.

He did not lock or even close his door.

He did not pace out syllables nor answer those who spoke to him. He skirted the market and climbed the small hill to the manor where it overlooked Baigan. The grand home sprawled: its tall stone walls were split by a huge gate of banded wood, but the yellow glow from dozens of paper lamps within still crept over the barrier.

The tower loomed nearby.

A black shadow against the stars, chill silence spread from its stones. He climbed the rough-cut steps to its twin doors. A rusty chain and lock were looped through the iron handles. Why lock the doors? Surely the tower was still to be manned; after all, boats and ships still sailed to the harbour.

He raised his hammer and smashed the lock.

From the manor came nothing but the drifting notes of court music played on flutes and the *biwa*.

Takashi ground the doors open and stepped within, boots crunching on gravel. The dark lay about his shoulders as a heavy mantle. He gripped his great hammer and hefted it. Here was the tower. Where the ants had directed him.

What lay within?

He turned to the wall and searched a moment—a lantern. He lifted it free and struck the lever, the little device shooting sparks. But light followed, a steady glow that lit a cluttered room. Tables and crates lay stacked beneath a winding staircase, but at the very back, behind a pair of torn screens painted with snow, something glinted in the light.

Steel? He moved closer.

Brass.

Takashi crossed the floor and shoved one of the screens aside. It clattered to the stone.

A large brass chest rested beneath a frayed blanket. It had slipped free so that the brass caught the lantern light. He pulled the covering aside. Another lock on the lid, but this, too, he smashed with his hammer.

And then he could not move.

Could not lift it.

Nor even reach forth to lay a hand on the cold, gleaming surface.

He exhaled; he'd been holding his breath, and his throat had tightened. There'd been no such moment for Shima or Kiku. Only the sweeping blue roaring of the ocean, waves tipped in white. Only a terrible absence coming home. He had to open the lid.

A yellow butterfly rested within.

Chou lay upon her side in the brass coffin; a great, dark bruise covered her temple. Her eyes were closed and her skin pale. No smile graced her lips. The stillness was complete; even his shadow seemed to shrink away.

"No."

She had deserved better.

Takashi spun with a cry as he hurled the lamp. It hit the wall with an orange burst. He strode back into the night, hammer held in white knuckles as he bore down on the bright manor.

And he counted syllables as he stalked.

*my spirit set adrift –*
*butterflies dance on*
*the autumn wind*

# Esmeralda

Thomas placed the final black stone on the burial cairn and stood back, shielding his eyes from the vicious sun. Faint trails of red dust whipped across the barren plain before the crumbling ruin. He sighed. *Is this all there is to the world, truly? Even here, so far from all the despair?*

"What is it, Thomas?"

Mia stood with her arms folded, sightless eyes staring across the desert, dark hair swirling in the breeze. Dust covered her vest and pants – even her hair bore traces of the fine red sand. Her willow-rifle rested against her hip, the slim weapon little more than a guide now, since they'd not come across any ammunition in weeks.

Thomas hefted their pack onto his shoulders, pot within thudding against his back, and moved to stand by her. He placed a hand on her shoulder and squeezed. "David said to follow the old river to *Esmeralda*, so that's what we'll do. He said she'll be able to help us."

Mia shook her head. "We don't even know what he meant."

"I know, but we have to keep walking."

She gripped the rifle and leant against his chest. "Don't be so calm all the time. We're in trouble, you big fool; we're running out of water and Williams is probably still following us."

He put an arm around her, sleeve riding up his forearm to reveal the ugly yellow hourglass tattoo. Borrowed time – the slave's mark. "King Williams is probably miles away. I doubt he even knew which way to follow."

"Don't call him that; he's no king."

"I know that too, sis." He sighed again. "Did you want a moment?"

She pulled back, offering a small smile. Her green eyes grew wet when she faced the general direction of the cairn. "No. I said goodbye when he was still lucid."

"Then we'll leave him to the sand."

Mia turned away, starting without him, the rifle clicking against the few stones remaining in the sandy earth. Thomas looked to the cairn once more, the ribbons of granite shimmering in the dark stone.

Beneath lay the only man who'd protected them, a bright man, a noble man in spite of his oft-times mischievous sense of humour. "I'm sorry, David," he said. In the end, the old fellow had been losing hold of the present but at least Mia had been able to calm him with her singing, usually an ancient lullaby. *Maybe we failed him today but not tomorrow. Whoever Esmeralda is, we'll find her.*

"Thomas!"

He spun. Mia stood a little ways away, feet braced, rifle gripped in her hands. Thomas ran to her side, sliding in the sand. "What's wrong?"

"I hear something. It's distant, but it's the sand-hog, I'm sure of it."

"Then that bastard has caught up with us," Thomas said as he turned a circle, scanning the horizon. A dust cloud billowed up behind the wavering heat-lines that marred the earth. "There's his dust."

"How far?"

He grunted. "Williams will be upon us by sunset. Maybe

before if they've guessed our path."

"Then we'd better hurry." She held out a hand.

He took it and together they broke into a jog.

~~

The giant blue sky was melting down to orange at the horizon; shadows crept across the sand as Thomas came to a halt, Mia pausing beside him. One shadow had seemed to be cast by an eagle or falcon but when he glanced up, there was no trace of any bird. Was the heat making him imagine things? The huge, twin-peaked mountain thrusting up from the flat desert was no illusion, however. Still distant, it was taller than... than anything he'd ever seen. It dwarfed the shells of the tallest buildings left behind by his forefathers.

He glanced over his shoulder; the clouds from the hog neared.

"I feel something vast," Mia said.

"A mountain, like two cupped hands rising from the sand," he replied. "I think there's something at its base, too. We need to get closer." He strode forward. Mia followed, her rifle still preceding her, searching for obstacles. But the sand remained clear as it had for the entire afternoon; stunted, thin plants were few and far between, and stones had long since disappeared.

That was, until they neared the base and Thomas slowed, boots scraping on harder earth. "It's an ancient wreck – a steam train," he said.

Black iron absorbed what was left of the light beneath the mountain's shadow. The train bore a dozen carriages, all battered; many lay on their sides, half-buried in generations of sand. Red powder collected in the chimney and the windowsills, atop the wheels, smothering coupling rods, cloaking doors and hand rails. He described what he saw to his sister. "It's long abandoned; it might be a good hiding place."

"What else do you see?" Mia asked, her voice holding a note of concern.

He scratched at his stubble. "Little. It looks like we can access the first two carriages but the engine is pretty damaged. Farther on, I see the hint of an old rail; must have crashed a long time ago."

She gripped his arm. "Then you see no-one?"

A chill crept across his shoulders. *She feels something – friend or foe?* "Why? Do you sense danger?" He put a hand on the crow-bar swinging from his hip.

"Yes. No. Both – I can't explain it; I sense age, towering age. Something... I don't know. Just be ready."

"I will be."

The wind had died down and the rumble of the sand-hog grew louder, but there was still time to conceal themselves. Better yet, the steamer's passage would obliterate their tracks. Thomas unhooked his makeshift weapon as he neared the first carriage, glancing back to Mia. "I'll check."

"Be careful. And hurry."

He nodded. Even though she wouldn't have seen it, Mia knew he nodded, just as he knew she would be listening for any changes in the wind, vibrations in the earth or anything that prickled her sophisticated senses. He almost chuckled. *Whoever she inherited that from certainly didn't offer me anything special.*

His boots sank into the sand as he climbed, reaching for

a handrail and hauling himself up to the door. The glass in the small square window was so thick and clouded with dust that it was impossible to penetrate. He gripped the handle and pulled.

Jammed.

Thomas applied more pressure, muscles straining. Still nothing. He set his crow-bar aside and placed his free hand on the carriage wall for leverage and tugged again. A screeching followed as the door shuddered open. Ducking away from the opening, he snatched up the bar and paused.

No sounds from within. Peering around the doorjamb, he saw little beyond the patch of light offered by the open door. Thomas glanced back to Mia. She stood as before, only now she hummed to herself. The ancient lullaby – the one she always hummed.

Behind her, the distant storm of red from the sand-hog filled the sky and the roar of its engines crossed the sand ahead of it. It would arrive before full dark.

*We're running out of time.*

He stepped into the stuffy room and moved to one side of the door. His eyes adjusted quickly. Rows of spacious seats, fabric rotted down to fragments, rested beneath dust-choked windows. Muted light fumbled its way within. Steel racks for overhead storage were empty even of cobwebs. Rodent droppings, these too, long-since turned white with age, covered some of the tables and the sand that filtered into everything littered both sills and floor.

He moved down the aisle until he reached another door, which he wrenched open. Beyond lay the half-buried walkway between carriages. The huge bolt and clasp of the couplings connecting them peered from the red. The second carriage was just the same, only darker.

Mia's voice called, words indistinct.

Thomas rushed back to the first carriage, pausing at the doorframe.

She'd climbed half-way to the carriage. "Well?" she asked.

"Nothing amiss yet. It might serve as a hiding place," he said.

"Good."

He took Mia's outstretched hand and drew her into the shelter of the carriage. "Do you feel anything?"

"Nothing new... wait, I think –"

"Greetings, travellers."

An old man with a white beard and faded blue overalls stood in the open door at the far end of the carriage. A shovel rested against his shoulder and a cold lantern swung in one hand as he approached.

"Greetings." Thomas did not remove his hand from the crowbar, but neither did he lower it.

The old-timer slowed, stopping a few seats away. "You two seem like you're pretty far from home."

"How can you tell?" Mia asked softly.

He chuckled. "This is the end of the world, so I suppose everyone who comes here is far from home."

Thomas blinked. "The end of the world?"

"Well, it might as well be. Nothing much beyond the Praying Mountain but red sand and then endless cliffs. You must be thirsty, the both of you. I have water with me, outside."

Thomas glanced to his sister. She had not moved.

"You can trust old Garrett," he said. "I'm not going to harm you – but you'll need my help to hide from the sand-hog, believe me. The *Esmeralda* is the only shelter for miles and miles."

Thomas stepped forward. "Wait, are you saying this *train* is Esmeralda? Not a person. Not a place?"

"Right you are."

"We've been searching for it," Thomas said. "The man who raised us said –"

"No need to bore him with our life story," Mia interrupted. "Can you really help us, Garrett? Do you have weapons, a way to escape?"

"Just who's chasing you, girl?"

Mia gave a slight smile, as if being called 'girl' were amusing. Thomas almost smiled himself – they hadn't been children for years now. *Maybe orphans are never truly children, anyway.* Not that David had been a failure, but there was always something missing. Some sense that he and Mia came from somewhere else. And the years before David...

"Heard of 'King' Williams out here at the end of the world?" she asked.

Two white eyebrows shot up. "That's some real trouble."

"Then you'll know he doesn't like it when his slaves escape," Thomas said, holding up a wrist to reveal the hourglass.

Garrett squinted before sitting on the nearest seat, a humph-sound escaping as he did. "You're both yellows, huh?" He set the lantern on the back of the nearest headrest. "That's a little more than I'm used to dealing with, I have to admit. Palace slaves usually don't get so far."

"But you'll try help us anyway?" Thomas asked.

"I will. It'll have to be the last carriage," the old man said as he stood. "Williams won't be able to get in. Once he searches the other carriages and finds them empty, he'll likely give up."

"Maybe, maybe not," Mia said.

"Well, you'll have to take that risk. No other trains to hide in."

"So how do we get in?" Thomas asked.

Mia frowned. "Or out?"

"I'll show you, but first we need the key," Garrett said with a nod to himself. He led them back outside – moving swiftly despite a limp – to the setting sun where he circled the relic's engine and climbed its steps, grunting with the effort.

"Are you all right?" Thomas asked.

"The knees go first, lad."

A boiler dominated the room; large enough to house a whole family. The door stood open, the hinges rusted, and broken glass in the copper pressure-gauge caught the light. Nearby lay a collection of shovel heads, arranged on a stack of crates, all empty.

"I took the few remaining handles for my camp," Garrett said when he noticed Thomas looking at them.

Garrett slipped into the cab and rummaged about in a tin box, muttering to himself. Thomas followed. The room was barely large enough for two. Copper handles reached his knees beside a wide seat, the bulbs on their ends worn. Through the dusty windows, the great wall of the mountain was darkening as the sun fell further.

"Here!" Garrett exclaimed. He held a heavy key up with a grin. "Thought I'd lost it."

Mia called from the boiler room. "That sand-hog will be here in moments, can we hurry things along?"

~~

As they passed the carriages, the old man offered them lukewarm goanna meat and water, which Thomas accepted gladly, despite craving a hot meal. Somehow, meat always tasted better right off the flame – even in a desert.

"We appreciate your kindness," Mia said between mouthfuls. "How long have you been here?"

"Months now." He wiped his brow. "There's old stories about this place, about what it used to be – holy land to the people who once lived here. I thought there might be treasure but I haven't found anything yet, bar a few cave paintings of snakes and lizards. And a giant bird; at first I thought it was drawn in gold paint." He chuckled. "I was wrong about that of course, but still, there's no time to shed tears over my rotten luck."

The last carriage rested some distance from the bulk of the *Esmeralda*, mostly up to its eaves in dark sand where it lay against the base of the mountain. The line of the long-buried train tracks curved in a half-circle, allowing a clear view of the train.

"How did it crash?" Mia asked. "This carriage is some distance from the others."

"Don't know, sad to say. Must have been a terrible day for the folks, so far away from help – this was well before the sand-hog and the like. Over a hundred years ago – pre-dates the Coal War, she does," Garrett explained as he climbed to the iron door. Its window, like all the others, was caked with dust. He brushed away a foot of sand at the base as best he could and inserted the key into the lock, ringed by an ornate brass sun.

When he swung the door open it revealed a second, heavier door, which was also locked. The same key admitted them into a large room lit by a narrow strip of light from where the roof had twisted free from the base; yet it illuminated little, leaving only an orange stripe on the wall opposite.

And more importantly, it was nothing anyone could squeeze through, by any means.

Mia gasped when she stepped inside and Thomas tensed. Danger? No, no. It hadn't been a gasp of fear... was it awe? Garrett knelt to light the lamp, winding a lever that clicked as it turned. Steady white light bloomed.

Thomas felt his own jaw drop open.

The room was full of caged birds. The light glinted on their steel wings and sharp beaks; the silver and gold plate alone had to be worth a kingdom, not to mention the gears and cogs that would surely lie within. Crystal gleamed in their tiny eyes, as if twinkling in sunlight.

All were identical.

"Robins," Thomas said softly.

"What is this place?" Mia asked Garrett. "I feel vast potential here."

"Allow me," he said, and led her to a cage. "It's not dangerous."

She reached in, lifting a robin free to rest within her palm. Her face was full of wonder as she ran her fingertips across the intricate body, her worry-lines easing. Thomas swallowed; his chest swelled. *God, how long since I've seen her face look like that?*

The old man gestured to the birds. "I think an old king was transporting these treasures. Who knows? But not a single bird works. I've even taken one apart and all its pieces are in perfect order. There's just something missing; they're worthless to me."

"I recognise these," Mia said. "At least, I think I do. Thomas, do you remember the story David told us about the Royal Mechanical Birds? They were built for young princes and princesses, to emulate real birds."

"And that's what these are?" Thomas asked.

"Why not?"

"I suppose so." He couldn't help a grin. "I'd much prefer if they were guns. Or a steam-car."

A low rumbling rose then fell, as if the nearing steamer had crushed half-submerged stone. Its reinforced sides and heavy wedge would have dealt quite easily with the obstruction but the sound was a timely reminder.

"Stay here and you'll be fine," Garrett said, handing the key over and heading for the door.

"Where will you hide?" Thomas asked. "You could stay here."

"Yes, stay," Mia said.

He shook his head. "If they do search the area and find my camp empty they'll be thorough instead of moving on. If they find me, I can send them on their way easily enough. They won't care about one crazy old man out in the desert."

Thomas frowned. "Williams isn't that reasonable."

"Don't worry, son. I have a few tricks up my sleeve. Now stay quiet, won't you?" He shut the outer door, which Thomas locked. Next came the inner door; its muted clang covered the sweeping that followed as Garrett obscured their tracks, muttering about his back as he worked.

Then his muffled voice grew distant and eventually the

growl of the approaching sand-hog smothered it.

"I have to see. Be my eyes," Mia said.

Thomas arranged a pyramid with a few of the square cages, placing them beneath the gap in the roof, grunting as he lifted the heavy steel. Then he climbed atop and peered into the orange light.

Outside, the sand-hog bore down on the *Esmeralda*. The beastly machine sat two-storeys tall, and poured steam and smoke into the dusk from twin boilers. Orange light flashed off the reinforced windows in the engineers' box. Portholes for passengers – or in this case, soldiers – were closed. In battle, the great beast covered them with heavy blast shutters, rendering it immune to any rifle. Thomas had seen the heaviest shot leave naught but a mark on those shutters.

While the hog wasn't agile, such deficiency was offset by sheer power. Gatling guns flanked the steamer's top deck and sides, the gunners' platforms outfitted with heavy shields. Unmanned – for now.

Garrett was nowhere to be seen.

The steamer slowed as it approached the line of carriages, hissing and sending a spray of red sand forth like a wave. The sand crashed over the *Esmeralda*, even the last carriage. Thomas flinched from it.

"What was that?" Mia asked, her voice tight.

"Just sand," he said, speaking softly. He straightened to peer back out. The new sand would cover any incidental tracks Garrett might have left too. Good. "The hog's stopped. The deck is still clear... wait, here they come."

A hatch flipped open with a clang that ricocheted off the mountain and rang across the desert.

Men in heavy flak jackets, with willow-rifles strapped

to their backs, climbed out and took up positions at the Gatlings, while others scuttled down ladders to fan out before the steamer. More and more men followed, until it seemed no-one could possibly reside within the steamer anymore. *Too many.* No soldier approached the train but a woman's voice boomed from the large brass tube beside the cabin.

"In the name of King Williams, show yourselves. You are property of his kingdom; hide at your own peril."

Thomas shifted position on the cage. The voice was familiar.

"It's Elisabeth," Mia said. "Williams sent her after us – too lazy to come himself. Maybe we're not that valuable after all."

"She's still his second in command," Thomas said. And an uncompromising woman, too. A crack shot and far too clever, truly, to answer to Williams. Thomas nearly shrugged. *She probably has her reasons.*

Silence crossed the space between train and steamer.

"You test my patience," Elisabeth called.

*No chance, lady.*

Yet after a time, movement atop the steamer caught Thomas' eye. Men were manoeuvring a bulky gun into position. *Damn thing's huge.* The barrel seemed to be several feet wide. A thin trail of steam rose from the body. At the weapon's rear, men shovelled fuel into a small boiler, shouting about keeping an eye on the gauge.

He muttered a curse – a steam-cannon. Maybe Williams did want them after all. But why? *We're not that special, are we? They've got dozens of slaves in the Fortress and they can get more any time they want.*

"What is it?" Mia asked.

"They have some sort of steam-cannon. I didn't know they were safe enough to use yet."

"Now we do," she said, beginning to pace a small circle. "I don't like this. Can you see Garrett?"

"No. I don't think –"

Cries from the hog cut his words short. A boom rang out, a great explosion of hissing steam following as the cannon rocked back on its rail. Its shot hurtled into the first carriage like a thunderbolt, leaving a smoking hole in the caved-in side of the *Esmeralda*.

"Come out now or we will break every carriage open. If you make us come in and drag you out ourselves, you will become slaves with no hands – should you even survive. Do you understand?"

Thomas flinched. His heartbeat quickened. He looked back to Mia, whose expression was stony. Was surrender really an option? Too many years enslaved before David rescued them. *No.* Thomas clenched a hand. He remembered the taste of dirt all too well. *I can't go back.* And neither could Mia.

Again, commands rose from the sand-hog and the steam-cannon was shifted to aim at the next carriage. Steam began to hiss until another explosion rang out, smashing through the steel and glass effortlessly.

"Any ideas?" Thomas asked.

"Nothing yet," she said before taking a breath. She hummed as she stepped, her soothing voice at odds with the tension in his body.

"Damn it." Thomas sat atop one of the cages, head in his hands. There had to be something – maybe if they made a run for it between shots? How thick was the sand, truly? Maybe the cannon wouldn't even break the double walls of the last carriage... or maybe it would.

A new voice joined Mia's.

Thomas lifted his head.

"Do you hear that?" he asked.

His sister stopped. "What?"

"Hum again."

Mia repeated the melody, a simple rise and fall to the old lullaby, and was soon joined by a light chirping. *A bird?* Thomas strode across the room, examining the cages. "Keep going," he said. If the birds weren't truly broken, was there a chance they could buy their freedom?

Another shot crashed into the next carriage, a piece of steel clanging against their hiding place. "Louder," Thomas hissed.

Mia raised her voice – singing the words now, and one of the mechanical birds twitched. Its wing fluttered as it turned toward Mia, and it too matched her song.

A second hopped in its cage, and then a third. New chirping filling the room until a dozen voices had joined Mia. Would Elisabeth and her men hear it? The lullaby was growing deafening now as the whole carriage joined in. He spun back to climb up to his perch, blinking against the light.

The men gathered around the sand-hog had not turned their way. Yet. But they were lining into formation; Elisabeth would soon send them to check the wreckage.

Mia paused to reach for him. "Thomas, you must close your eyes."

"Mia... what?"

"Please, I felt it before, I can call it to us. I can save us."

"What do you mean?"

The birdsong had swelled to an unpleasant pitch. Every single bird sang now, beaks flashing in the bright light... *Bright light?* He turned back toward the gap in the roof but an incandescent brightness from outside stopped him. He swore, ducking down to cover his head with his arms.

"Don't look until I tell you it's safe," Mia shouted over the song and then rejoined the chorus, her own voice soaring.

Thomas squeezed his eyes shut but the light bled into his mind.

Within the blackness of his eyelids a searing heat bloomed. A great white bird flared, wingtips aflame as it bore down on him.

Its beak opened in a shriek and it swept down to crash in an explosion of stars.

Something rocked the carriage walls.

Thomas flinched, but there was only the gradual fading of light and then silence, a silence soon broken by a soft sobbing. He opened his eyes, slowly. Then he lifted his head. The brilliance of the fire-bird was gone but a soft glow lingered, sneaking into the last carriage.

The mechanical birds had fallen silent.

Mia was weeping.

He stumbled to her, taking her face in his hands. "Mia, what..."

Mia's tears were streaked with blood and her green eyes stared directly into his own. "Thomas... I can see your outline," she said, and her smile was radiant. "You're fuzzy but you're there."

"I... *how?*" He barely spoke above a whisper.

"The Great Bird," she said, and then turned from the light. "God, it hurts so much more than I expected."

The bird of fire... or light – what was it? A deity once worshipped by the people Garrett mentioned? Those who hadn't left any relics behind? Thomas took his shirt and tore a strip free. "Here." Gently, he tied it around her head, covering her eyes. "Is that better?"

She nodded.

Thomas exhaled. "What now?"

Mia took his hand. "Now we leave, before the ones inside the steamer find us," she said.

Thomas paused to listen. Cries of despair and fear rose from outside. Voices shouting for help, shouting in pain. Confusion. Terror. He swallowed when he made out the words. "They're all blind," he said.

"Yes."

And finally something else dawned upon him.

His sister had called the bird of light; his sister had made the dead machines sing. Mia had used... magic... somehow. He exhaled. Magic. How? And what did it mean? Was that the reason Williams hounded them? Two slaves who'd been on the run for years? *Did David know all along?* Once again, Thomas wished there was someone who could tell him just who their parents had been.

Why they'd abandoned him and Mia.

And yet, as it always did, the question he could never answer only hardened his resolve. Mia had to be protected – that hadn't changed. Her vision might be restored but it was clear Williams would never stop chasing them.

Thomas looked back to Mia and smiled. *And I will never let him take her.*

# Dust

It was still a city.

Perhaps that was supposed to make a difference. More opportunities for decent food and clean water. For money – which meant something here. Was it the safety in numbers thing? Alana sniffed. Or the flimsy certainty that concrete and steel could really hold back the howling emptiness of nature.

She passed through a jagged hole in the rear of a warehouse wall and into a dust-choked street. No movement beyond the stirring of yellowed weeds in the sickly breeze. They pushed through the bitumen with abandon and she narrowed her eyes, checking her facemask almost as a reflex. But here the weeds bore no purple splashes, no deadly spores.

"Small mercy," she muttered.

This far on the city outskirts, buildings were blocky sentinels of their former selves, windows and doorways gagged by boards and refuse. Graffiti – whether of paint, blood or faeces – ran across the concrete in stripes. Anti-outsider, anti-government rationing, anti-bloody-everything.

Maybe 'city' was a stretch – it probably used to be one. Was it Yarra City? No signs anyway. But whatever the name, it was closer to the harbour, closer in turn to New Albion and its airport. Closer to true freedom.

Colour flashed in a doorway. Alana swung her rifle around. No more than a rag caught on a nail. She eased the weapon down and exhaled. *Steady.* No point wasting a shot, even one bullet could make a difference.

The farther she walked, the more evidence of life slithered forth. Rooves in place and thin smoke drifting from chimneys. Fewer holes in the streets, glass in windows. Streetlights – though cold for now – but neon signs pulsing from the shadows between buildings. Voices, too, rose from within the homes and shops, quiet arguments or bartering for medicine or drugs perhaps.

Ahead, a truck rumbled through an intersection; painted black and fitted with scuffed bulletproof Perspex. Government riot police, all holding automatic weapons, clung to the sides like Redback spiders.

None looked her way though.

She crossed the street, heading for the green-glowing sign of a chemist. The grimy door was hardly welcoming but she nudged it open with her foot.

A radio hissed static, broken by occasional reports from a racetrack. A memory grazed her – the sound of an announcer calling horses – but those days were long gone. Only dogs ran now. A muted glow came from the counter where a man leant on its glass top. He wore a modified gasmask; bug-like eyes wary behind the Perspex.

"I don't sell to ten-cent-heads."

Alana sneered. "I really look like a user to you?"

He straightened, folding his arms as he did. "Can't always tell."

"You barter? I'm looking for clean water."

"One litre for your rifle."

She dug into her jacket and removed a nugget of gold, twisted like bad bread frozen.

The man shook his head.

She replaced it. No surprise; no-one had been willing

to take it, it was almost worthless. "What about this." She placed a flash drive on a keychain. The plastic was battered but it was intact.

He leant forward. "That thing work?"

"Did a month ago. I tested it in Southbay. It's up to date – get you inside."

He reached out, hovering over the pass a moment, as if afraid to touch it. It was probably worth a little more than the water but she didn't care. "Why'd you leave?"

"How about that water, buddy?"

"Fair enough." He scooped up the USB stick and disappeared into a back room.

She leant against the counter and tapped her boot. A tiny figurine of Yoda, one ear missing, sat by a dusty log book. The writing was little more than scrawl to Alana; it didn't look like English or even another known language. It was some sort of hybrid. The radio droned on.

"Want to speed it up?" she called.

No answer.

"Hey!" Alana snapped. Still no reply from beyond the door. She gripped her rifle upright as she circled the counter and paused to listen at the door. Scuffling from beyond. What was this guy up to? She took a breath then kicked the door open, bursting after.

A figure loomed from the shadowy shelving. She rammed the butt of the rifle into it and the shape collapsed with a grunt. Light flashed and she sidestepped, squinting as she stumbled against a shelf. The light followed her and she raised a hand. "What the hell is going on?"

"Business," the chemist said. "You gotta survive somehow."

Alana levelled the rifle at the light. "I don't mind spending a bullet on you."

Something wet closed over her mouth and nose. An arm crunched her against someone's chest. She thrashed against her captor. The fumes were thick, slowing her responses.

"Hold her still," the chemist snapped.

A jabbing pain in her arm followed, cold spreading through her veins.

Darkness.

~~

Slowly, a bright light resolved above her. Ugly fluorescents warmed only slightly by a lamp. She twisted her head and her stomach flipped, a wave of nausea on its heels. Only indistinct shadows. She lay atop something cold and hard. The scent of antiseptic filled the space... *Shit, this looks bad. Where am I?* The chemist! Alana strained against her bonds but they only dug into her wrists and ankles.

She shivered, goose bumps forming across her exposed skin.

Both jacket and shirt were gone but her bra remained. Her jeans and belt too, even her boots. So why remove only some of her clothing... Stitches ran along her side, crimson seeping between coarse black thread.

"Oh shit."

Had they taken her organs?

"The anaesthetic will wear off soon," a woman's voice announced from behind Alana. There was a dullness to it, as though she was missing something. As if, when she spoke, what issued forth was a recording of her own voice, not the real thing. "I am impressed; you are the first to regain consciousness."

The first? How many had *not* woken? What the hell had they done to her?

Alana tilted her head.

Only the woman's hands were visible at the edge of the lamplight. They were lined with rings of all types. Jewels, silver, gold, even bone and something plastic too – a toy like the ones found in old vending machines. The nails were ragged, as if chewed upon, the skin wrinkled. But it was clean too and the glimpse of fabric they rested before revealed an impeccably clean burst of yellow.

"Let me go."

"I mean to. You have a task to complete."

"What are you talking about?" Alana strained against the bindings again. No looser than before.

"Save your strength; you have to share it now."

Babblings. "Give me a straight answer, will you?"

"You are young and strong. I need your body." The hands spread, as if to better show the deep wrinkles. Did black ink swirl within the veins, or was Alana seeing things, her vision still swimming? The shadows faded. "You can save my son," the woman said.

"How?" Alana sneered. "By giving him one of my kidneys? You piece of shit. Same goes for your chemist friend."

"Be calm," the old woman said, her dead-voice unperturbed by Alana's outburst. "I have taken nothing. And Reginald did only what he had to in order to survive. Of course you judge him – yet I have seen your rifle. Will you tell me you have never used it to protect yourself?"

"I don't need a lecture. And –"

"And I will give none." The woman moved closer, still not

close enough to reveal her face – only the tip of a red scarf now. "I have also seen the passes you carry. Three in your name, including one for New Albion. Access to a utopia in our crumbling world."

"To hell with your son," Alana shouted. Rage and panic coursed through her body. "What have you done to me!" She needed the Albion pass; it'd taken a goddamn year to earn it.

Her captor raised a finger, a ruby catching the lamp-light. "A complicated procedure. As I said, I've taken nothing, but you now carry my son. You will sustain him on the trip to Albion. He will not die here in this cesspool, not while I have breath." A hint of emotion entered the voice now and at the same time, it seemed ink swirled beneath her knuckles.

Alana shuddered. It couldn't be true. How? Was the woman talking about artificial insemination? Or something else? A twinge in her side. Did the stiches quiver, or was she trembling? Blood trickled in a pencil-thin line down her skin. No. The old bat was lying. Alana glared back up at the woman. "Let me go."

The woman receded into the shadow. "Your possessions are in the next room. When you are freed, I expect you to head immediately for the river to buy passage to New Albion."

*Agree and just get out of here.* "With what?"

"You will be provided for."

"Fine. Untie me."

Silence.

Alana strained her neck, trying but failing to pierce the shadows. "Hey!"

Steel ground over tiles. Heavy footfalls neared and a figure loomed over her – a man. His beard buried most of his face and his eyes were sad but he did not speak. He produced a knife and she tensed, but he only bent to cut her first hand free and then the other.

"Who are you then?" she asked as she tried to rub feeling back into her wrists. "The hired muscle?"

"There's money in the other room; money for the ship and for you."

"Payment for what your freak of an employer did to me?"

He did not answer, only turning to free her legs. "Take the passes and drugs too, you'll need them."

~~

Even fully clothed and armed once more, half a dozen streets from the walled mansion, walking a little gingerly, Alana couldn't rid herself of the sense that the old woman was watching, her dead voice a rasp in every step. Yet the only other people on the street this late were not interested in her. Most of the neons were dark now, offering only electric blue claims of Water Purifiers or a few pink brothels, leaving none but the guttersnipes and drunks. The Snipes knew she had nothing to offer and the drunks were busy emptying their stomaches – they were more the Snipes' style. The few alert men that gave her a second look quickly changed their path when she let the rifle clear of her long coat.

She needed to find a real surgeon or a doctor – someone better than the predators in Yarra City. There was still a proper hospital in New Albion, maybe there. Yet *there* was just where the hag wanted Alana.

*Not that I have much of a bloody choice.*

Her side ached and pulsed in time with her heartbeat.

Pain grew as the drugs wore off. She'd have to take another pill, one of only four she'd found with the money – she'd stumbled into more money than she'd ever seen. Enough to buy that flight to another country – a goddamn clean country. But only *if* she could get to the airport in New Albion, four days travel on the river. Still, the ship first.

And then, once she reached New Albion, the hospital, to find out what the old woman had really done. The story about her son was beyond ridiculous. It was insane; the bitch was fucked in the head.

A stabbing pain shot through Alana's abdomen.

She stumbled, hand to gut and sucking in a breath at the pain. It subsided swiftly. Strange. Or sinister? Alana strode on, one eye on the signs above doorways, the other on the shadows between streets. A breeze had picked up, dragging plastic pill cases and beer cans like orphan children.

Her hand went to her face-mask. Still in place.

Up ahead, a Wayfarer's sign struggled to fend off the night. It was the kind of four-walls-and-one-bed, no-heating hotel she'd have used in the past. But with the money she'd been given, maybe something a little better was in order. Something with a bath – maybe she could wash away the violation she felt.

Alana shivered as old, wrinkled hands seemed to caress her skin.

The Single Season had several rooms left but nothing on the ground. Still, Alana took the fourth floor room and bolted the door behind her after paying. The cost had been exorbitant – the price of wasting clean water on bathing. Recycled stuff was more traditional, but the cost was barely a dint in what the hag had given her.

Alana tossed her pack at the foot of the bed – a single blanket and pillow only, but spotless all, even the carpeting. She drew her bath, glancing out the window into the darkened street while she waited. No movement this close to dawn.

Steam enticed her from the other room – the automated cut off not far behind. Alana undressed before the narrow mirror, pausing before she could remove her underpants.

The stitches were moving, as if something slithered beneath her skin.

She choked on a gasp and squeezed her eyes shut. *God, is it real?*

When she opened her eyes, all was still.

"God damn it." It had to be an after-effect of the surgery or drugs. None of the pills came with packaging or markings, just two white circles left in the plastic bag. She hesitated... should she take another? The pain was growing again.

And she was thirsty too.

*After the bath.*

Alana took a flask and sunk into the hot bath with a sigh, her hallucination not enough to totally dampen the wondrous feeling of full-immersion in clean water. Tomorrow everything would look different. She had money, a real chance of reaching the airport, a chance at something she'd hadn't let herself believe truly possible in years.

Freedom from desperation. Clean air, untainted water, untainted and more than enough for everyone, water that you didn't even have to buy! And food that tasted of the old flavours, rather than the bitter mush that was common fare, things she hadn't tasted since childhood.

Despite the cramped conditions of the tiny bath, Alana

emerged with muscles looser than they'd been in weeks. Maybe months. She ate a little dry fruit then checked the door and window before collapsing onto the bed.

Her dreams were muddled sketches of water; a waterfall, a pond, a riverbed, the ocean.

~~

Alana lifted her shirt to check the stiches.

They were already falling out. She was healing far too quickly. What had the old bitch done? Gently, Alana probed the skin around the long incision.

Something pushed back.

Alana bit back a shout. Something *was* inside her. She moved her trembling hand toward her flesh but could not press down again. A bulge rolled beneath her skin, as though something had twisted within. A child? *God, no.* There was no way. Something else. A fucking tapeworm or what?

What sick game was the old woman up to?

Alana ran to the bed, snatched up her pack and rifle, and headed for the stairs. Her boots clapped against the concrete steps, one hand on the rail. Two flights down and the shouts of men arguing floated toward her. She slowed but the voices receded when a door slammed.

On the street she ran, feet pounding, the echoes swallowed by the growling of engines as another jeep full of government soldiers passed. One of them men swivelled his head toward her, eyes unclear behind the mask. They did not stop. The red stripes were like a vivid slash of blood against their black uniforms.

She had no idea where she was running; any direction

was good enough, so long as she kept moving. Kept putting metres, blocks and kilometres between her and that woman.

Something *twisted* within her.

*No.*

Alana pushed ahead, stumbling now. She slumped against a cold wall to catch her breath. *Get it together.* She had to reach the harbour. The ship might have already left. Alana ground her teeth as started forward again, soon approaching the docks.

Black iron gates, sick with the malaise of rust, towered over the thin line of passengers. A squad of soldiers were searching the people. She glanced to the haggard buildings either side and there too, were men in black, holding long rifles. Doubtless there were other snipers she could not see – anyone stupid enough to attempt to force their way onto the ship would face hail of armour-piercing bullets from half a dozen angles.

The man queued before her wore fine leathers and a company logo on his mask – some sort of desal-plant, it seemed. Twin handguns hung from his belt and his eyes were disinterested when he glanced at her, soon turning back to the gates.

Her hand crept toward one of the guns.

Alana tensed, eyes widening as she fought to control her limb. It was straining forth now. She clamped a hand over the wrist and dragged it back to her side.

And then the fight was gone. She had control once more.

A nasty flash of pain in her side followed – a message, but one she hardly needed. The stitches were on her left side. Her left arm had been the one she'd lost control of. God knew what was inside her. *Is it feeding on my insides?* Would it devour her from within or would it one day take control of her entire body? Alana clenched her fists, fingernails digging into her palm. *No.* She had to get it out.

The man before her was waved through the gates with barely a glance and the soldiers checked her pass before directing her toward the office, where she paid a squat, spectacled man her fare and kept on toward the river cruiser. Once, it had been a mighty red and blue but the paint had long since faded and gone streaked with age, like generations of pale vomit slipping over the side. Steely moss had colonised the bottom, nearest the waterline. Two men in heavy overalls clung to the sides, blasting away the poisonous moss with oxy-torches. Many of the windows were boarded up but enough caught the noon sun to reflect, to give the ship the illusion of vitality.

Despite the weathered appearance, it was solid and a giant to boot – more so than the other boat she'd been on in the past. A steel staircase led up to the decks, crowded with drab-clothed passengers and the occasional soldier. Or, those who were fleeing the city, bulky collections of their possessions strapped to their backs.

A grey-uniformed boy with a scanner met her on the decks, checking her flash drive before directing her toward a stair. "That way, lady." It led down to what she hoped would be a clean, dry cabin. The few passengers ahead spoke in muted voices, but there was a suppressed sense of excitement to the tones. Hope, perhaps.

Jealousy surged up her throat; at least they weren't running from something forced into their own bodies.

Her room was smaller than she'd expected, even considering she'd lowered her expectations, but it was clean.

A porthole and a bed and basin – grey water only, she'd have to buy her drinking water of course – still, it was enough. A tool to get her one step closer to a doctor and then the airport.

She checked the door, lay back with her hands beneath her head and closed her eyes. Pressure grew in her abdomen. It was expanding within her. The discomfort quickly grew into pain. She sat up with a wince and lifted her shirt.

Protrusions strained against the skin. They were narrow, with regular ridges, and they moved slowly. Was it chewing on her abdomen even now? Alana clenched her fists, doing her best not to drive one of them into her abdomen. *Get out, get out, get out!*

The pain eased and the ridges faded.

She stood. Maybe there was a doctor on board.

~~

No doctor travelled aboard the *River Queen*.

One of the officers showed her the first aid room, where a pale green curtain hid a cot and a cabinet. The cabinet held rubbing alcohol, scalpel and gauze pads, a few rolls of bandage. A bin sat beneath the sink, the mottled floor evidence of an old, slow leak. She drew the curtain, removed her top and set the kit on the cot beside her. Then she dipped the scalpel into the alcohol and paused. *Steady hands now.*

She set the point of the blade to her skin and applied pressure –

Bright blood welled but Alana stopped.

Now wasn't the time. If she made a mistake or the... thing was difficult to remove, wouldn't it be better to have help? To have access to the hospital? And more, what if the old woman's 'son' was coiled around her organs or something worse, what if it wasn't even human? A fear she hadn't yet admitted to herself but could hardly deny. *You slimy prick.*

Alana exhaled slowly then replaced her clothing but pocketed the scalpel and took the kit, just in case she changed her mind. There was still three nights on the river, who knew what might happen?

The first night she left her room only once for the evening meal, purchasing hard bread and a typically tasteless stew. Still, it bore what seemed to be chunks of meat floating in the bowl. On her way out of the quiet mess hall, she purchased an extra litre of clean water, catching someone watching her as she drank, her thirst returning swiftly.

In her room, Alana locked the door, removed her mask and lay across the bed, waiting for sleep, since there was little else to do on the river cruiser. The view from the porthole was uninspiring and she wasn't going topside to watch the same sludge and blasted fields slide by, even though the chance of a clear breeze was tempting. Not that it would be that clean, but just to feel it on her arms...

Somehow, she slept – dreaming of an airplane leaving the dying nation far behind, spearing into a clear blue sky, silver glimmering... but the image was soon replaced by a clear blue riverbed.

When she woke, an ache deep within her, Alana drank an entire flask, frowning at a new tightness to the skin on her face. She rummaged around for the small mirror in the kit.

A green pallor covered her skin.

Alana shivered. Poor light or something else? She moved

to the porthole – no, it was no trick. There was a green tint to her neck and face. Dark shadows spread beneath her eyes. Inky veins.

Her eyes were wide in the mirror. It took a moment for another change to register; her fingers; a thin webbing now crossed from finger to finger. "Oh, God."

~~

Alana fashioned a hood from a cloak, purchasing string from a man in the orderly docks of New Albion. In the dawn light, he hadn't seemed to notice her sickly pallor. But it would only be a matter of time before someone did, mask or no. The tint was spreading to her hands. She needed gloves – or better, medicine, magic, anything!

Albion bore no rumble of troop-laden jeeps this early, nor the hum of whatever commerce it promised. If it wasn't just the softness of dawn brushing the broad streets, she would have sworn the place was cleaner than Yarra City too. At an intersection she paused on the pock-marked asphalt, leaning against the wall of what seemed to be a bakery. She nearly went inside – how long since she'd had sweet pastry?

Though she could have afforded it she found hunger had abandoned her – instead, she was thirsty again.

And besides, a less pleasant task awaited.

She needed to find the hospital – boarding an airplane in her present state would never happen. Didn't matter that she had a pass and enough money. *Not with this filthy thing inside me.* She swallowed, the thirst increasing. She sipped from a flask, glaring at the nearest passerby from beneath her hood but the man did not approach her, despite the way his eyes were drawn to her flask.

"Never been this thirsty," she muttered as she returned the water to her pack.

The tallest buildings were shells, becoming eyeless faces, the higher they climbed, but the lower floors seemed to be functional; these were government forts or the surviving corporations – the water hogs and the pigs who locked down medicine or technology. One of them had to be the hospital, surely.

The man within the bakery gave her directions, for a price, and she was soon standing before the hospital, doing her best to ignore the stitch-like pain in her side. The building was nothing like hospitals of old; no white walls and glass spanning from ground to sky, but more like a converted library with fluted columns and a ramp cut into what had once been steps.

A stooped man was exiting the open doorway when she crossed the threshold, heading for the desk. A woman in a dark, water-proof clothing rustled when she stood to greet Alana. "Good morning. How can we help?" she asked. She moved around the desk, walking with a limp. Belted at her waist was a taser – Alana hadn't seen one in years.

"Yes, I need to see a doctor," Alana said. She swallowed, having to force the next words out, as if her tongue were larger than normal. "Or a surgeon."

"Forgive me for asking, but our services are rather costly. Can you offer any manner of collateral or down payment? Something more valuable than your rifle – which must stay with me, I'm afraid."

"I have money," she said after swallowing another sip of water. She lifted the flask. "And more of this."

The nurse nodded, accepting the gun when Alana handed it over after only a moment's hesitation. "Very well, follow me to the examination rooms."

A steel-lined room with a cot and basin awaited her – she'd barely put her belongings in the corner when a slender man in a white coat entered. "My name is Doctor Alfred," he said. "I understand you're unwell?"

"Yes." She removed her hood and mask. His eyes widened but he only retrieved glasses from an inner pocket and leant closer, a slight frown on his lips.

"Have you been exposed to anything unusual of late? Toxins perhaps?"

"I think something is inside me," she said, lifting her shirt to show the scar. "Someone did this to me. I can feel it move at times."

He hesitated but bent to peer at the skin. "An old wound?"

"Recent," she said, frowning at the scar. It did look old today – a pale white line.

"Excuse me, miss?"

"I said it's recent," she replied. "Days old."

Dr Alfred stood. "I'm having trouble understanding you – slow down a little."

"I'm speaking just fine."

He removed a tiny light, holding it up to her eyes. "Have you had a head injury lately? Your speech is quite jumbled."

Alana opened her mouth to answer but no sound escaped. She swallowed and tried again, but still nothing. A third attempt won her naught but a gasp. Her pulse quickened. What now? God, if she couldn't even speak... Dr Alfred had already turned back the bench, making notes.

When he returned, she gestured to her throat, then the

pad and pen, miming that she wanted to write. He flipped the pad and extended both items. Her left hand snatched the pen and drove it into his neck where it met his collarbone. Crimson spurted forth. He fell back with a cry and Alana cried out. "No!"

She fought her whole body now – not just her left arm – as the *thing* writhed within her, yearning for death. Was it because the doctor might actually be able to help? *Bastard creature!* It was going to ruin everything. Her muscles locked and sweat formed. Footsteps were rushing down the hall. Dr Alfred had stumbled into the basin and was fumbling within a cupboard, one hand attempting to stem the blood.

The nurse burst into the room. Her expression of shock was replaced by anger and she had the taser free and aimed at Alana in a single motion. "Don't move, lady. This has enough volts to do more than slow you down, got it?" She turned her head. "Peter, are you all right?"

The struggle with Alana's own body ceased. The nurse was still watching, but checking on the doctor who continued to rummage around. Another weapon or something medicinal? Alana breathed hard. She was running out of choices.

*Try something, idiot.*

Alana leapt forward. She twisted, knocking the distracted nurse's hand aside and sprinting into the corridor. A shout came from behind but she only ran harder, clearing the building and thundering down the stair.

Water.

Glistening and cool.

The same riverbed from her dream, sun rippling across the surface. Clean blue, nothing like the sludge that passed for rivers nowadays.

The vision swam before her, overlaying the footpaths as she ran, straight and true. Coupled with the image was an urge to find the river. *Home.*

A crack split the air.

Something bit into her calf and she crashed to the ground. Alana rolled, scrambling for cover in a doorway. Drab figures in the street scattered. She peered around the doorframe, back to the hospital, chest heaving. The bullet was a burning star lodged in her flesh.

The nurse stood at the top of the ramp, Alana's rifle in hand.

An impressive shot. "Shit."

Alana tore part of her makeshift hood for rags and tied the pieces around her leg, gritting her teeth. She wouldn't be able to cover much distance without help. She swore, dragging herself up and stumbling down a side street.

Where now?

The riverbed reappeared, clouding her sight.

"No chance in hell," she told the thing within her through gritted teeth.

She scraped to a halt as one side of her body turned toward the river – but she fought it. "I said no!" Maybe she still didn't understand what the thing within her was, but she knew what it wanted.

And it would not win.

It was trying to steal her body. It tried to take her voice and now her dream of escape – her god-damn future too! For there would be no flight now, not as she was. No paradise free of decay and betrayals. Alana dashed a tear from her eye. Years of struggle wasted! Everything she'd sacrificed just to get this close, just to get all the way to Albion itself and be denied. Even if Alana weren't empty-handed, wounded and miles from the airstrip, the thing would seek to kill all who stood between it and water.

The selfishness was inhuman in its purity.

But there was one it could not kill. One it still needed.

"And you got the wrong host, buddy." Her grin stretched her skin and she poured all her hatred into it until her cheeks seemed to freeze in place. If she couldn't have a future then neither would the hag's pitiful son.

Revenge was all she had left.

Alana dragged herself deeper into the shadows of the city, further from the direction of the river. Every step was its own battle but she hissed, spat and fought until she came across a couple in a dusty four-wheel drive.

She caught the windowsill just as the man fired the engine.

He flinched and the woman sucked in a gasp.

Alana tried to plead for help but no sound emerged. Still the creature tried to stop her.

"What do you want?" the man frowned. Was he worried about her appearance? Worried that she was contagious? His beard was streaked with silver and he bore a spiral tattoo on his cheek. Ex-mercenary probably.

She pulled the last of her money free from her vest, a princely sum, and pointed toward the wastes to the west of the city. Then she pointed at her chest, then back to the waste, trying to convey her desire with a look and a shake of the money.

The driver's eyes lit up and he reached for the cash. "Get in back."

Alana hauled herself into the tray with a grunt, slumping

between heavy sacks of grain. Or maybe rice, her vision was still smeared with images of water. The pain in her body grew – spreading across her stomach, it was snaking around her very insides, squeezing.

She coughed up phlegm, leaning across to spit over the side.

*To hell with you.*

She lay back, staring up at the scuffed white and blue of the sky, ignoring the pain.

Each bump in the road sent a shockwave of agony along her leg but after a time, she no longer felt it. The sky rolled on. Once, near dark, she thought she caught a glimpse of lights high above – the airplane? A flash of bitter pain at the thought. It was too early for stars.

But it was growing dark. She blinked. Already? She lifted herself up and squinted into the dusk, wind pulling her hair free – naught but dust in every direction. The road itself was narrow and straight, disappearing into the horizon. No tree or shrub lined it. The only thing close was a blackened stump in the middle distance.

Alana thumped on the roof of the four-wheel drive.

The vehicle rumbled to a halt and she climbed out, wincing as her bad leg gave way. She caught the tray. The man and woman watched her in the mirror.

"Are you sure this is what you want?" he called over idling engine.

Alana raised a webbed hand and started walking.

Soon after, the man put the vehicle into drive, roaring away. She didn't turn, she just kept walking. There was a rush of desperation from the thing and the pain in her gut drove her to her knees but she crawled onward, gripping whatever rock she could use to pull herself deeper into isolation. *I'm not turning back.*

When darkness settled across the waste, she found herself in a shallow depression and finally lay back, exhaling heavily, the air chill across cracked lips. And so it would end beneath a sky empty even of a whisper of starlight; but she had won.

*And now we die together, you piece of shit.*

The thing inside her barely stirred.

*Drown in dust.*

Shades

The kid slouched at the mouth of the alley, ragged hoodie stretched over her taut frame. Blue light from the tattoo joint cast an ocean-like haze over the whole street. She lifted her chin as Leo approached. *She's got the punk attitude down.*

"You selling?" Leo asked.

She nodded. Her mascara had run, like her eyes were bleeding, but she stepped into the alley then opened her jacket without hesitation. Little plastic bags were clipped to the fabric. More hung from her skin-tight body suit, a riot of colour. The handle of a blade poked from the top of her heavy boots, a four-leaf clover on the pommel. "I've got some new Shades. There's an orange that's almost gold; it'll blow your mind."

He shook his head, both at the offer and the amount of illicit drugs she had. Far, far more than a typical dealer carried. "I'll take a Yellow."

Now she raised a pencil-thin eyebrow. "Would've taken you for a Pinker."

"No shit?" Leo ignored what she probably meant as an insult. "How much?"

"Forty." Her voice jagged on the hard 't' sound.

Leo grunted as he produced his card. "Prices go up again?"

"Sure." She lifted her own card. As they lined up, both pulsed green. "Syndicate's always putting their prices up." She handed him the little bag, yellow chip secure within, and he started back for the street. A gust of wind stopped him at the alley mouth; it carried empty fast-food wrappers like a silent train of decay.

"Hey, buddy, I gotta ask, what's with your face?"

He turned back to the dealer and grinned, despite the words slicing into him. "You only get one face, right?"

"Huh?" She frowned, as if the question were bizarre. "Dude, just go to one of the –"

"Thanks for the stuff." He pulled his own coat together and started up the street, breath steaming before him. Hoverlines slid by, glued to the adjacent magnetic strip. The nearest traffic light blinked its bastardised Morse code and each vehicle reacted as one.

At his drooping apartment building, he flashed his card before the door, which admitted him with a swishing sound. On the way upstairs, he passed a neighbour. Guy only offered a distrusting glance from the smooth valleys of his sculpted face. *Dime-a-dozen movie star face at that.*

Inside, Leo hit the entry light – which turned the tiles white, and part of the grey slate benchtop in the kitchen but nothing more. He tossed his coat aside, found the armchair and slumped into it. By the dim light he slid the panel on his wrist open, removed the Yellow and inserted the chip. At a flick, the little bag fluttered down to rest with the others, like a new carpet.

Then Leo closed the lid and lay back.

The shadows of his ceiling were quickly replaced by a simulation: he was sitting at a park bench with a couple of guys. Both mid-thirties, both laughing – laughing at something Leo had said. One was in construction, the other a music teacher. The chip fed that and so much more into Leo's mind, intimate details too, like the fact that Will, the teacher, was hiding an affair with his principal.

Leo *knew* them.

They were his friends. And they were *happy* to see him.

Over the meal they talked the regular crap you discuss on a lunch break – but the subjects didn't matter. What mattered was that they looked him in the face and didn't flinch. What mattered was they listened when he spoke.

~~

It was the weekend.

Which meant coffee injections in the *Stormy Cup* on the corner.

Romantic name for a joint with a line of scuffed seats facing the old harbour and where the vials came with a sneer and no-one had used a cup in a generation. Same as every weekend, but the *Cup* stocked the old brands at least. Leo cracked the casing and breathed in the scent of coffee – simulated, but better than the rest. He lifted his shirtsleeve and took the injection.

Real high point.

He reached for another vial but let it drop to the table.

Will was walking from the diner.

His hair was the same blond, close-cut, same ultra-bright blue implants in his eyes. It was him – the guy was even wearing the red jacket from lunch. "Holy shit." Leo leapt up, slamming his knee into the tabletop before storming after the man, who was already heading toward the harbour.

A heavyset fellow in a wet apron blocked Leo at the door. "You haven't paid, pal."

"I just need to see if –"

The owner gripped his arm. "Card, freak."

Leo glanced out the window. Will was already gone. "Fine." He tore his card free, lifted it and waited for the green pulse before shoving his way outside, ignoring the muttering that followed.

In the street, Will was no-where to be seen.

Seagulls squawked.

The wind fell away and the sun warmed Leo as he stood and stared.

*Mind's playing tricks on me.*

There was no way a real person would look exactly like a simulation, no way. It was just some sort of glitching echo, some fragment stuck in his system. Leo strode to a busier street and flagged down a hoverline, heading for home and then bed – best to sleep it off if he could.

~~

The next day he saw Will in the kitchen, making toast, and called in sick.

~~

Rain misted the streets as Leo searched for the dealer but he found only gleaming stones where she'd stood before. "Damn it." He stepped into the tattoo parlour, walking a short corridor lined with examples of the artists' work, prices and bold claims – *The New Ink* even worked on human skin.

A pretty woman whose face seemed nothing more than a web of signatures sat behind a glass counter. Her eyes widened in shock as he neared, but a smile and a cheerful greeting followed. "Need some ink, pal?"

"I'm actually looking for someone."

"Someone who works here?"

"No. There was a girl out in the alley. A dealer. Do you know her?"

"Not really." She lowered her voice. "But if you're looking to score some Pink or Red, I can fix you up."

"No. I need to know if she was passing bad chips." *Because if she isn't, there's something seriously wrong with my head.*

The woman lifted an eyebrow, quickly lost beneath her fringe. "Yeah? Hmmm... maybe that's why she's gone."

Which made sense. Either that, or she was on the run. After all, she'd had a *lot* of chips yesterday. "Who'd know?"

"You really want my guess?"

"Please."

She flipped a phone into her hand and tapped the screen. A hologram snapped up, revealing a vintage orange slidecycle on a sign. Initials rode the tank. *K&W.* "If you want to take your life into your hands, find that shop in the old quart."

"Thanks." He turned and started back down the corridor. The syndicate was bad news but no simulation had ever bled into his waking mind before. And it wasn't like he could ask a friend for help.

Leo hurried along the streets, pushing through raincoats and their plastic owners at busy intersections. A block from his place he slowed; Will, dressed in the same red jacket, stood up ahead.

"This is a bad idea, buddy."

Leo blinked.

"Just what do you think the syndicate will do if you waltz in there and start asking about one of their dealers."

"I have to know," Leo replied, keeping his voice quiet. Nearby, a man walking his mastiff frowned at Leo. The dog passed through Will without reacting.

Leo glanced ahead, spotting a little garden, and hurried between the open gates. Inside, he passed the replica fir trees and found an empty park bench.

"What's the rush?" Will asked.

"It should be obvious – I don't want people to see me talking to myself."

"Fair enough."

He hung his head. "God, why am I doing this?"

Will put a foot up on the seat and leant over his knee. "Doing what?"

"Talking to a hallucination. A freak result of a bad chip; it happens you know." *At least, that's what I hope it is.*

"Not all the time."

"That's not the point." Leo jabbed a finger at Will. "The point is, you're not real."

"Does that make my advice bad?"

He rubbed at his eyes with a sigh. "No, it doesn't."

Will was gone when he opened his eyes.

~~

K&W's Vintage Cycles spread across a corner block, a single replica gas pump out front and the same orange slidecycle hanging above the doors. He paused a second, took a breath, then entered. Both Will and the girl in the tattoo shop were right; he was taking a serious risk.

*No risk, no gain.*

Dozens of bikes confronted him, from new, sleek

magnetics to the classic slidecycles, and off to one side, beneath fancy down lights, a hog with actual wheels. *Echoes of the Hells Angels here.* Up the back, two men were playing cards at a desk; one was a heavy-set fellow with a big beard – going for ruggedly handsome – and the other man thin, with slick black hair.

The slick guy stood as Leo approached, an expression of distaste clear. "Help you?"

"I'm looking for a dealer."

Slick sniffed. "So find one. We sell cycles."

"A specific dealer, actually. I hear this is the place to see about that."

"Hey, I get it," Slick said, coming around the desk with a smile. A cattle-prod hung from his belt, the tip sharpened to a gleaming point. "Even ugly ducklings need cyber-pussy, and you're the ugliest duckling I ever saw, but this isn't the right place for you." His smile disappeared. "So fuck off, already."

Leo took a step back. "Look, I'm not some strung-out Pinker – I think the dealer's passing bad chips. If she's yours, I thought you'd want to know. And I'm trying to get my money back," he added, hoping it'd be the kind of thing they'd expect.

Slick paused.

The bearded guy set his cards down. "You want to describe this chip-hopper?"

"She's skinny and wears a hoodie. I saw her near *The New Ink*, it's a tattoo shop," Leo said, and the bearded guy was already nodding.

"Gina works the ink place. You say she sold you some bad stuff?"

"Right. Hallucinations. A Yellow."

Slick frowned, glancing over his shoulder. "You know, she hasn't checked in since last night."

The bearded man tapped a meaty hand on the desk. "Call her and scan him."

"What?" Leo looked from face to face.

Slick pointed. "You stay right there, Frankenstein." He was pacing, tapping his temple lightly as he did. After a moment he swore. "She's off-line."

Beard's expression darkened. "Him next."

Slick strode to Leo, but did not raise his prod – instead, soft green cells slicked over his eyes while he stared.

"Shit, Dennis, you should see this guy," Slick said. "He's like ninety percent flesh. There's a mod for illegal chips and implants for broadcast signal and that's it. He's only on the grid as a static unit."

Dennis grunted. "Is he a cop or not?"

"I'm just looking for Gina." Leo raised his hands. "That's all."

Slick's eyes returned to their regular brown. "He's no narc but he's probably handled just as many chips."

Leo flushed, but he had to ask Gina if other customers had experienced glitches since he didn't fancy pushing Slick or Dennis for more info. "So can you help me?"

Dennis stood. "Listen, friend. If you think a vat of flesh like *you* can find her you're stupider than you are hideous. She's off-line and you can't even Glide."

Will appeared beside the heavy, a sad expression on his face. "I know where she is. Get yourself out of this and I'll tell you." He flickered as he disappeared.

Leo licked his lips; no-one else had heard Will's voice.

"Ah, maybe you could recommend another dealer?"

Slick put a hand on his prod but Dennis stopped him. "Now, now, Ronnie. Let's not turn away a customer." He smiled, revealing impossibly straight teeth. "Mac works the solar farm, check it out."

"Thanks." Leo turned and strode from the shop and into empty streets, soon stopping in the dank recess of a doorway. "Will?"

The hallucination appeared, red jacket open. He wore a State Capital Ravens shirt. "I'll tell you but you have to ask her something, right?"

"Fine."

"Ask her how about the Valley."

He frowned. "Where's that? And why?"

"Trust me." Will held out a piece of folded paper. "And good bye, Leo."

Leo took it and found a handwritten address within; a place in the mountains. "Will, are you sure –"

The footpath stood empty.

~~

Leo parked his rental before the shack, cutting the beams.

The afterimage of a small hut huddled between pale tree-trunks lingered like a lightning strike. It had been a rough ride – the roads out here weren't kind to hoverlines but now he had a chance to figure it all out. And while he'd still ask, he didn't *need* Gina to spill about her chips to prove his sanity. For that, he only needed to open the door.

If Gina waited inside, he wasn't crazy.

If the joint was empty, he was.

That simple.

And that terrifying.

*But that's what you get for following hallucinations.*

"Gina, are you in there?" he called as he approached the door, now lit only by moonlight. No good freaking her out any more than he already had with his arrival; she probably thought no-one knew where she was. And she probably had more than her knife now. "My name's Leo; you thought I was a Pinker. I'm not here to hurt you or anything. Can we talk?"

Silence.

"It's about your chips. I think maybe I've been hallucinating. Have any of your other customers had the same problem?"

Still no answer.

He swallowed, nearly at the door now. "I don't even need to see you – but if you could answer… I'd know I'm not crazy if it was just the Yellows, you know?"

"You alone?"

His heart flipped. "I am."

The door opened a crack, a military grade taser pistol leading appearing before Gina's thin face followed. Her eyes widened a little at the sight of him. "You?"

"My name's Leo."

She opened the door enough that he saw her shrug. "I mean, yeah, a couple guys came back but they took a refund. That what you want?"

He smiled, a weight detaching itself from his shoulders. *Not crazy. That feels pretty damn good.* "No, it's fine. I just needed to know."

"Well, it probably was so you can chill out. And leave, all right? I came all the way out here for a reason, you know."

"Because you stole half your inventory."

She glared at him. "So what if I did?"

"I don't care that you ripped off the syndicate... just hope everything works out."

"Sure," she said as she shut the door.

"Wait," Leo said, resting a hand on the wood. "There's something else I wanted to ask."

"Hurry it up."

"Do you know a place called the Valley?"

"Nope."

So much for Will the Hallucination's important question. "Right. Well, thanks anyway."

Leo returned to the hoverline and climbed in. No matter; he had what he needed. It had been the Yellow after all. Just a few more days of glitches then everything would be back to normal. He gripped the steering wheel. Normal. *Which is what exactly?* Working the call centre by day, then spending all his money chasing the rainbow so he could slip into simulation every night? *Man, your whole life's a fucking simulation. Why don't you search your phone service again, Leo? See if five years worth of stored silence is still waiting – I'm sure the company will humour you this time too; pretend they lost a message here and there.*

"Hey!"

Leo jumped in his seat. A shape ran toward him; Gina. She leant against the driver's window, tapping on the glass. He slid it open. "Gina?"

"I remembered something," she said. "I knew a girl from a place called the Valley. She was like you. Kinda ug – ah, no enhancements, you know? She was pretty strange. Refused to get her limp fixed. She said it was against her people's way of life."

"Her people's way of life?" Could it be real? A place where no-one cared about upgrades and endless primping, a place where no-one would give him a second look? "She ever say where it was?"

"Somewhere across the twin rivers, I think."

Wild country out that way. Leo glanced at Gina. "You know, I bet a place like that, where they probably don't have much tech, would be a great place to hide out."

"I guess so." She glanced over the roof, back toward the hut. "It's funny you asked me about the Valley, you know."

"It is."

"Seems like a real lucky guess?"

"More like a hallucination from the Yellow."

Gina pursed her lips. "You know, I realise something. Those guys that came back for their money? They weren't buying Yellows."

A little shiver ran through his body. "What?"

"Maybe it's a sign that we're meant to cross paths." She gave a shrug.

"I like that better than being crazy."

"Tell you what, how about we talk about it on the way to the Valley?"

"Huh?"

She started toward the hut, calling over her shoulder. "Just let me get my stuff."

Leo sat back in his seat, shaking his head, but he was smiling despite the confusion he felt. *So this is what I'd forgotten; the hope you feel at the start of a friendship.*

He glanced up to the bright moon. "Thanks, Will."

# The Boy who Breathed Disco

Eric's waiter was sour milk.

Not just the man's expression, but his complexion too. Even the whites of his eyes were off. And the way he held the menu, puffing his chest out. Was this guy trying to prove something? An electric candelabra sent light bouncing off the brown panelled walls, heavy potted plants and onto the waiter's greying hair. He wasn't elderly – and yet, he was still old enough not to do the whole macho posturing thing, wasn't he?

Or so Eric thought.

Eric grabbed a second menu and pointed. "No. Here. I'd like the carbonara." The candle on his 'table for one' flickered as someone left the restaurant. Inoffensive 80s AOR was lost momentarily, as the roar of traffic elbowed its way in.

"Sir, you'd enjoy the mushroom soup."

"Maybe, but I'd like the pasta."

The waiter glared down at him. "You'd like the soup better."

Eric blinked. Not sour milk – his waiter was crazy. It couldn't be a joke either, because, well, jokes were funny. The man's jaw was clenched. What sort of waiter got shitty when a customer refused the special? How fucking special could it be?

He stood. Time to get another waiter.

The floor was empty. No other waiters, no sign of a manager. In fact, only one other table in the restaurant with customers. A young family; the little ones, two girls, clapping their hands, pigtails bouncing. Their parents murmured together; there was a glaze to the woman's eyes that spoke to the kind of deep weariness he'd seen on his sister's face. Two kids under five.

"Where are you going, sir?"

As bad as he wanted pasta, it wasn't worth it. Should've stuck to the pizza place, got something delivered. "Home, mate."

The waiter skipped around the table, pushing Eric back into his seat. "You should stay." He didn't raise his voice, but his arms trembled. "I can make it ugly, if you don't."

What the hell? Eric shot up, fists clenched. If this bastard wanted ugly, he could oblige. "How about I –" He stopped, glancing over his shoulder. The girls. They didn't need to see him beat up a waiter. Why ruin their night?

The waiter grinned, as if he'd followed Eric's reasoning, and knew he was safe. "So, Mr. Slater, will you be taking that soup now? The chef will be most pleased."

Eric nodded, sitting down. "I'm sorry, yes. That'd be great."

The waiter weaved through the empty chairs, heading for the kitchen. The moment the doors swung shut, Eric got up and left.

~~

Eric leaned forward in his chair, forearms on the cool steel of the cafe's outdoor setting. He shaded his eyes, despite the canvas umbrella above.

Across the road, between hulking department buildings, crouched the restaurant from last night. Dark cars, roaring trucks and bikes obscured elegant white letters crowning the double doors. *The Gentleman's Rest* was closed. Admittedly, it was early and maybe the place was too far from the CBD, but so was the cafe he sat in and it was open. And it held the generic hum of conversation typical to all cafes.

"What are we doing here? I thought you had to teach."

Ben scratched his jungle of hair. A laptop sat open on his side of the table and he typed with one hand.

"Not till next week," Eric said. He took a sip of vanilla milkshake and pointed. "You ever eaten there?"

"Nah."

"I'm thinking of making a complaint. Last night this waiter tried to force me to change my order, then shoved me into my seat when I wanted to leave."

Ben snorted. "Really? What the hell?"

"I agree."

"So what are you waiting for? And what did you need me for? I thought this was lunch."

Eric grinned. "I was hoping you'd order for me. I'm going to run over there."

"Fine." He resumed typing, shaking his head at the screen.

Eric jogged to the crosswalk and tapped a foot, waiting for a break in the traffic. Maybe it wasn't just about making a complaint. A creepy joint. It wasn't until he got home last night that he'd realised the waiter had used his last name. Eric hadn't phoned ahead to make a reservation. Just walked in on impulse.

Lights changed and he crossed, heading to the door and trying the handle to *The Gentleman's Rest*. Locked. He peered through the glass into blackness and chewed his lip. "That'd be right."

Was there a back door?

The service lane was rich with graffiti. Pinks, purples and yellows in a riot of mating, and slumped against it all, piles of garbage. Flies patrolled black bags of brutalised lettuce and lumps of things straining against the plastic. An industrial bin had one lid open, the other flat.

The door to the rear of the restaurant was open but Eric paused. A voice hummed, coming from behind the bin. He crept forward. It was *Rikki Don't Lose That Number*, intercut with coughing.

A middle-aged man in a rumpled suit, filthy with pasta sauce and crushed bananas, lay against the wall, his bed of garbage close to drowning him. His eyes widened and he stopped humming. "Don't go in there. You're the boy who breathed disco. They want you."

Eric gaped. His mother called him that. Claimed he was born on the dance floor at a disco, a week early. The DJ had stopped the music and held her hand while Eric's father helped with the delivery, then rushed them to the hospital.

"Who the hell are you?"

"Listen to me, I know. Don't go in there." Trash-man wheezed. "You can't trust them."

Eric stepped forward. "How do you know me? And who are 'they'?"

"The chef told me about you, but I know everyone, boy. Now turn around and walk back to the street. You don't trifle with *The Gentleman's Rest*. It's like an old spider web."

"You on drugs or what?" What a waste of time. "Who's the chef?"

"She's the one in the chequered jacket."

"And she knew my mother?"

Trash-man wheezed a laugh. "I never said that. I said,

'Don't go in there'."

Eric shook his head and strode into the restaurant. Time to find out what the hell was going on. His footfalls echoed on the tiles. A toilet door flashed by and then he was flinging a door open. A clean kitchen waited. The sour waiter stood at a bench lined with chopping blocks and knives, and turning at Eric's entrance, was a tall woman in chef's whites – only the jacket was chequered.

She blinked, and for a split second her eyes were mirrors, but her smile was right behind. "Welcome, Eric."

He hesitated. Had her eyes really been actual mirrors? They were blue enough now, too wide to make her face traditionally attractive, and yet he stared.

She stepped forward, placing a cloth on the bench as she glanced over her shoulder. "Oliver, I think we'll have a classic. Crème brûlée."

"Grand idea, madam."

To Eric, she smiled again. "Everyone loves crème brûlée, right?"

"I'm not hungry."

She was close now, her long hands held together before her. "You'd make me happy, if you ate with us. We've been quite lonely, and we hardly know the city."

Eric shivered. His stomach was slow-churning, a spin cycle through mud. He retched. Something poured from the woman, something *wrong*. He backed into a wall, but she kept on. Dark hair curled at her neck, the ends frayed.

"How do you know me?"

"You're the boy who breathed disco, that's enough for me to know you." She reached for his cheek but, he pulled his head back.

The turmoil in his stomach had not lessened. Sweat formed at his temples and he swallowed a tide of nausea. What was happening? Food poisoning? The chef's eyes bored into him and his stomach gave another lurch. Her lips were so pale. She was mesmerising – and hideous. And there was no doubt, she was causing the nausea. No way was he sick. He had to get out.

Eric ran.

"Oliver, stop him."

Eric tore open the door and stumbled into the hall. Footsteps thundered after him, but he burst into the alley and onto the street, arms pumping. He looked back only once.

Oliver stood at the mouth of the alley, hands on hips.

~~

Eric sat on an armchair, phone in hand, back to the wall of his dark unit.

No lights. And the TV? No chance. A glow from the front unit pushed through the curtain but he kept out of it just in case. One of the neighbours was having a party, a chorus of drunken voices scattering the hush of night.

He'd rushed home from *The Gentleman's Rest*, forgetting Ben, and burst into his bathroom where he grabbed the basin and heaved the contents of his stomach onto the porcelain. Then, he'd stumbled back into the lounge to collapse on the couch, falling into a welcome sleep.

Awake now, he kept an eye on the door, dialling again. "Come on, Mum. Pick up."

"Hello?" A voice croaked.

"Mum, it's me."

"Eric? What's wrong? It's so late."

"Ten pm I think."

She laughed. "Well it's much later here. Now, what did you have to wake me up for?"

"Something a little strange happened today." More than a little. "I met a chef, a woman, who called me 'the boy who breathed disco.' Do you know her?"

He could imagine her pursing her lips before she answered. "I don't remember knowing any chefs really. What's her name?"

"She didn't say. But she had wide-set eyes." He closed his own eyes, trying to keep his voice casual. "You'd remember her."

"Nothing's coming to mind, darling. Why do you want to know?"

"It just seemed strange that she knew that story."

"Oh, I must have told that story to hundreds of people over the years."

"What about Dad, did he know any chefs?"

"Not that I can remember."

Nothing. Maybe it shouldn't have been a surprise. "All right, thanks mum. I should let you get back to sleep."

"You get some sleep too. You sound tired."

"I am I guess."

Her voice changed. "Are you looking after yourself? I don't want you running yourself into the ground."

"I won't. Love you, Mum."

"All right. Love you, too."

He hung up and dragged his feet to the bathroom. So how did the chef know that story? He shrugged. Could they be stalkers? But why? He didn't have anything valuable and he sure as shit wasn't famous. He shook his head. Time for a shower. His breath was rancid and when he ran a hand through his hair, his fingertips came away greased with old sweat. He stripped off, kicked his clothes at the washing basket and stepped into the shower, turning the hot water on hard.

If it got hot enough, maybe it would wash the chef's gaze from his skin.

Time passed in a haze of steam. When he finally got out of the shower, he chucked a towel on and brushed his teeth. Twice. Still dripping, he moved slowly through the darkened rooms to the kitchen. He needed *Nutella*, straight from the jar. He took a spoon from a drawer and opened the walk-in pantry.

The spoon clattered to the floor.

*The Gentleman's Rest* lay beyond his pantry door. The entire restaurant stretched before him. Tables were set beneath the chandeliers, and from the kitchen's entry, Oliver smiled across at him.

Eric slapped his own cheek.

Nothing changed. The restaurant remained. Its music drifted into Eric's kitchen and soft voices followed, from a couple at a nearby table. They were smiling at each other, the man tracing his finger along her palm.

Oliver started forward and Eric slammed the pantry shut. He scrambled back, thumping into the sink. The tap squeaked when he turned it and he splashed his face with water and turned in a circle. "What the fuck?" He crept back to the pantry door and reached out, hesitating.

What if the restaurant was still there – was he crazy?

He pulled the door open.

"Good evening, Mr. Slater." Oliver stood with an arm outstretched, gesturing to an empty table. "Dining alone, I take it?"

Eric slammed the door and ran, stumbling through the lounge room. In the hallway, he snatched at his car keys and then he was out the door, slamming it too and slamming into the bonnet of his car where it lurked in the driveway.

He jumped in, jammed the key into the ignition and stomped on the pedal. Shooting from the driveway in reverse, Eric nearly killed one of the partygoers. He ignored the man's drunken cursing as he wrenched the wheel, spinning onto the road and shoving the gearstick into drive, before tearing up the street without looking back.

~~

His sister Katie gaped at him from her doorstep, her dressing gown and slippers matching blue. "Eric, what are doing here? And where are your clothes? You look like garbage."

"I need somewhere to hide." He shivered, not just because he was cold, keys in one hand, the other keeping his towel around his waist. "Something's happening."

Her face darkened. "Come in here."

"I'm okay," he said. "I think."

She led him into a warm lounge room. Deep armchairs were arranged around the TV and the carpet scattered with giant Lego blocks. Katie sat him down, tying up her blonde curls as she did. She reached for a cigarette, taking a drag. The little red light glowed – a fake. Water vapour hissed from her mouth. "Tell me what's happening. And keep your voice down too. You could've woken the twins."

"Sorry. Where's Dan?"

"At work. His turn for night shift." She put the cigarette down. "Come on, what's going on?"

He kneaded the towel. She wouldn't believe him. No-one would. How was he supposed to tell her a restaurant was stuck inside his pantry? Just like the scene from *Ghostbusters*, only he didn't have a proton pack or Bill Murray's composure.

"Eric, let go of the towel. Tell me what's going on. Is someone after you?"

He unclenched his fists. "All right. Just try and hear me out, until I get to the end."

"Go ahead."

He sighed before launching into the tale. He started with the waiter, then the return visit and the man in the trash who'd known about his birth, the chef and her strange gaze – the one that caused him to throw up – and finished with *The Gentleman's Rest* appearing in his pantry. "And that's why I can't stay there tonight."

Katie stared at him a moment, a slight frown creasing her forehead. "Eric, why don't you sleep here and I'll call a doctor in the morning. It sounds like you're hallucinating, especially with that pantry."

He shook his head. "I didn't imagine the man in the alley. Or the aggressive waiter."

She took his cheeks in her hands. "How do you know, honey? No-one else saw any of it."

"I just know." A tear squeezed itself from his eye. "Otherwise, what's happening?"

"Look, spend the night down here on the couch. I'll make

you a nice breakfast and tomorrow... tomorrow we can take it from there. I'll get you a pillow and a blanket."

"All right. Thank you."

She stood. "That's what big sisters are for."

"Calming potentially delusional, half-naked brothers on their couches in the middle of the night?"

She spoke over her shoulder. "That's exactly what we do."

~~

The whole thing seemed stupid the next day.

He sat on a stool, spooning cereal into his mouth. The milk chilled his teeth, but the warmth of Katie's house made up for the shock. Morning television nattered away in the background, clashing with the squawk of her children. How blessedly normal to sit in a kitchen and eat breakfast. Even wearing Daniel's clothes, jeans and a collared shirt, he was almost plain old Eric again. Much better than terrified, rasping Eric.

"Hold still, girls." Katie made a clucking sound. "Ten o'clock, Eric, all right?"

He turned on the stool, smiling at the girls – who peered at him over their shoulders as they stood to have their shoes tied. "Ten o'clock," he said.

"Can you find the place ok?" She hoisted Sara onto her hip, taking Jasmine's hand and leading her to the door.

Eric hopped down after them. "Don't worry about that."

She gave him a look. "All right. Just ... call me after, ok?"

"I will. Bye, girls." He waved them off, grabbed a drink and locked up, before slipping into his car. The sun was hot for so early in the morning. He wound the window down and the scent of lavender drifted from the garden.

He could go back to the house, check the pantry. Be sure. Then he wouldn't have to wait until ten to see if he'd been hallucinating. Or he could drive by Greene Street, visit *The Gentleman's Rest* one more time. Demand some answers.

"Worked out fine last time," he told the dashboard.

Eric turned the key and the engine growled, as if unwilling to wake. He revved it, pausing with a hand on the shift. Ten o'clock was too long and Greene Street on the way home.

He pulled out of her driveway and rolled through the seminal manicure of the suburbs; Katie had found the template upon which all suburbans streets were founded. By the time he'd made his way into the city and pulled up half a block from Greene Street, he was sweating.

Eric got out and locked the door. He checked the handle twice before kicking the tyre. "This is bullshit." No time to be timid. What had the chef's eyes done to him?

He stormed along the footpath. Ahead, an old man strolled along, a bunch of flowers held behind his back. Eric skipped around him but skidded to a halt at the intersection for Greene Street.

*The Gentleman's Rest* was gone.

In its place stood a laundromat, cute bubbles on the sign. He spun, then looked back. Had he got it wrong? No, there was the cafe he and Ben ate at.

He stopped the old man. "Excuse me. Can I ask you a question?"

A white moustache covered his mouth. "Yes?"

"Can you see that shop over there? It's a laundromat, isn't it?"

He squinted. "I'd say so."

"Thank you." Eric let him go, crossing the street in a trance-state. The world was going to bat shit. No-one could swap a restaurant for a laundromat overnight. Where the hell was *The Gentleman's Rest*? He bypassed the doors, slipping into the alley. If Trash-Man was still – Eric stopped.

The big bin, the black bags of rubbish and Trash-Man were gone. The alley was cleaner than some kitchen floors he'd seen.

He ran.

~~

Ten o'clock and his appointment came and went as Eric sat in the car, staring at his front door.

Sweat clumped his shirt. Traffic hummed and the radio fuzzed *Riders on the Storm*. He had to smile. What a dull scene for a movie; it needed an explosion or something. He switched the radio off. If he went inside, would the *Rest* still be within his pantry? If he never opened the door again, would it just stay there? Oliver and the chef, trapped with the packets of pasta, cereal and half-finished bag of Milk Bottles.

Sitting in his driveway wasn't solving jack.

He got out. Trash covered the lawn, as if each party goer from last night had vomited something as a parting gift; beer bottle, can, cigarette stub, cigarette pack, actual vomit, chip packets, it was all there.

His front door was closed at least; he sure as hell hadn't locked it when fleeing in his towel. There was every chance one of the drunks from next door had got in. If one of them was passed out inside, he'd wake them up with a good kick.

Then check the pantry.

Eric flexed his hands. In we go, let's see what's inside already.

He opened the front door and stepped into ... *The Gentleman's Rest*. Eric shook his head and blinked, hard. Who knew that squeezing your eyes shut could actually hurt? When he opened them the restaurant was still there, still mostly empty. No Oliver and no chef, just the same couple and their kids from the last time.

He spun, tearing at the door handle, but the doors were locked. Eric kicked the wall.

"Hey, buddy, relax. They're shopping." The man had stood, and was waving him over. His wife bent with their kids, tickling them. "Take a seat."

Eric lowered himself into a chair. The man's wife smiled before turning back to her kids. Something about her cheer seemed a little forced, as though she was pushing through bone-deep weariness, perhaps.

The man extended his hand. "I'm Michael. This is my wife and our girls, Isabel and Rose."

"I'm Eric." He shook Michael's hand. "What's going on here?"

"*The Gentleman's Rest* is stalking you, isn't it?"

"You too?"

Michael's eyes clouded. "Not anymore. But we're making the best of it."

"Wait, so you can't leave?"

"No. But you probably can. You haven't eaten the soup yet."

"That's how they got you?"

Michael nodded, eyes turning to his wife, who only smoothed her red dress.

Eric stood. "We'll, they're not forcing me. Let's go. I'll help you."

"I said we're trapped." Michael shook his head. "And so will you be. Just accept it."

"Well, fuck that, Michael, because I don't have to accept." He turned to the girls. "Sorry."

Eric ran for the door and yanked on the handle.

"It only opens when they want it to," Michael called. Did the poor fool sound satisfied?

Eric took a step toward the kitchen, then froze. Oliver appeared in the doorway, his hair aglow. "Mr Slater. You look hungry."

"Fuck you, Oliver."

The man's face hardened. He advanced, a giant pepper shaker in one hand. It looked heavy enough to do some damage. Eric strafed the dining room. Michael and his family did nothing, said nothing. Anticipatory hush ruled.

"Sit down and eat something, Mr Slater. Perhaps some soup?" Oliver quickened his pace.

Eric bumped against the window. A way out! He snatched a chair and spun, hurling it into the glass.

White snow exploded.

Oliver roared as Eric dove through the shattered window and crashed onto soft lawn, rolling to his feet. The front window of his home gaped open. Glass fell from his hair when he stumbled back and a warm trickle of blood ran down one forearm. "Wait..." He crept forward to peer through the broken glass but saw only the shadows of his furniture.

He stuck his head inside. From the next-door neighbour's place a question floated over, but he ignored it. The lounge was his lounge. Grey carpet littered with glass, but everything else as it ought to be. Book left on a coffee table. TV quiet.

Eric climbed inside and crept to the kitchen. The door to the walk-in pantry stood waiting, slats still and handle frozen. He knocked on it. Oliver didn't answer. He lay on his side and peered between the bottom of the door and the cool tiles. Darkness.

"Hell with this." He rose with a grunt and tore the door open.

Shelves of food, cans and packets of pasta, bags of flour and sugar. No restaurant. Eric collapsed in a lounge chair. His house was ... infected. As if *The Gentleman's Rest* had leeched onto it. Shattering windows instead of using doors every day of his life wasn't a solution either. He fumbled for his mobile and rang a glazier, organising repairs. The guy wasn't due to arrive for a few hours, but same day repairs weren't too bad.

The restaurant left him little choice. If it followed him home, could it follow him to other homes? Katie's was out of the question. Same with Ben's – every place was out of the question, really. And he couldn't even strike back. The joint was a brick ghost. If it wasn't in Greene Street, it could be anywhere.

He straightened as he muttered, "But that's still enough."

If the damn place was everywhere, all he had to do was try doors until he walked back in. Only this time, he'd be ready.

He dialled again, tapping his finger on the armchair until Ben answered. "Eric, what's up?"

"Ben, do you still have your Dad's gun?"

~~

He met Ben in his friend's driveway, motor running. Ben frowned at him from his step, coffee mug in hand. "You going to come in? Or get out of the car?"

"I can't, Ben. It's something I'll have to explain later."

He walked across the front yard. "It's not about that restaurant is it?"

"It is. But don't worry. That's why I want to borrow that gun."

Ben blinked. His expression was a sudden tribute to *Dumb & Dumber*. "What?"

"So do you have that revolver?"

"Yeah, but what do you want it for? And it's actually Dad's old shotgun, Eric."

Quick. Make up a good lie. "Someone from the restaurant broke into my place."

"What the hell?"

"It's in case they come back." Inside he groaned. Crap lie, Eric. "I've already been to the police; they can't do anything unless Oliver from the restaurant comes back and they won't post a guard, that's for sure."

"That's crazy."

"I know. But this guy's insane. He thinks I got him fired, for harassing him at the restaurant."

Ben frowned. "You're that worried?"

"He smashed my front window." And God, what a prick, what a liar. Sorry, Ben.

"Shit. I'll get the gun, then."

~~

Eric gave up opening and closing doors in his house and drove through the city.

It had to be somewhere.

That fucking restaurant was toying with him, but he'd fix them. They'd back off or be sorry.

The faint glow of a petrol station appeared on a corner. His tank was due. Time to fill up. Then another few laps, maybe check Greene Street again. He pulled up to a pump and killed the engine. The gun gleamed where it rested on the backseat. Using a hacksaw in his bathroom, he'd sawn the barrel so he could conceal it beneath a dark trench coat. He even took the time to file it and had an apology ready for Ben.

Only now, about to fill up and pay for petrol, did it become clear. He'd transformed himself into the classic criminal. Dark coat, sawn-off, angry and alone... shit, he had it all. He was a fucking joke.

But what choice did he have? There was no way he was going to let the *Rest* take everything and no way the cops would help. No way he'd involve Katie and her family, no way he'd involve his friends. And he couldn't leave the gun in the car, what if someone saw it? Broke in and stole the damn thing. He tucked it inside his coat and filled up. Did the butt bulge? If the clerk – a sleepy-looking old guy – freaked out, the plan was out the window.

Stay calm, idiot. That was all he had to do. Stay calm and pay the attendant, get back in the car. No problems there. He clicked off the bowser and headed for the sliding door.

He controlled his features, glancing at the old guy.

Just walk up to him and – tables and chairs, dim lighting, Michael and his family talking over their meal.

*The Gentleman's Rest.*

He shook his head. "Of course."

"Eric, do you see what I mean now?" Michael said, looking over.

"Yeah." He strode toward the kitchen, flinging the doors open. Oliver was already crossing the white tiles, but the chef was no-where to be seen.

"That's far enough, champ."

Oliver froze, eyes narrowed. A pot of boiling soup ticked away behind the man.

"I've decided that I want you, your chef and this god-damn restaurant to disappear."

"Mr. Slater, we cannot do that. We've only just arrived."

He kept a grip on the gun. "Then I kill you two and leave anyway."

"Do you?"

Could he? He turned the gun on the soup and squeezed the trigger. The pot exploded and the recoil drove him back. He nearly laughed – was it delirium?

Oliver said nothing.

Eric pumped the gun, spent shell clinking across the floor. "So, where's the chef, then?"

"Right here," the woman said. She stood in her chequered jacket before the storeroom door, which he hadn't heard open. Her wide-set eyes were unafraid. "And I must say, what a pleasant surprise it is to see you." The sense of wrongness exuded from her, though it didn't seem quite so strong this time.

He levelled the gun at her. "Since you're in charge, I'll tell you what I told him. Back off. I want you and your restaurant to disappear."

"Or you'll blow us to pieces?"

"Exactly."

"Murder, Mr. Slater?"

He shook his head. "I've made my point. And now I'm leaving. If I see either of you again, lights out." He turned to the door.

"Take him, Oliver."

Eric spun.

Oliver charged across the tiles, face impassive. "Get back," Eric cried. The man closed with him. Eric snapped the gun up and pulled the trigger in a cold reflex. A boom followed and the waiter flew across the room, blood exploding.

His shredded torso slid to crash into the bench, leaving red smeared across the tiles.

"Oh, fuck."

The chef sighed, but didn't appear more than mildly annoyed. "Stay there, Oliver. I'll start defrosting another one."

"Yes, ma'am." The man's expression was one of irritation, blood splatters covering his chin. He was just as unperturbed as his boss, who stepped into the storeroom before Eric could move. Or blink. Or breathe – he exhaled, hands shaking.

"What the hell is going on?"

Oliver didn't answer, and after a moment, the chef returned, dragging a frost-encrusted body in a waiter's suit by the shoulders. She dumped him with a thud and wiped her hands on her jacket.

"We'll just let him thaw out first." She smiled at Eric.

"Want to see what will happen if you shoot me?"

He gaped.

"Just accept it, Eric. Your place is here now. We've chosen you to become part of something ... different to the regular world. You're special; you could help us grow."

He swallowed, still shaking his head. "I'm not interested."

She moved closer. He raised the gun and she stopped. Maybe she truly didn't want to be shot, despite her confidence. "Eric, we could be happy. I can promise that."

He backed away. "I don't think so." He sprinted for the doors, kicking them open. The chef gave chase as he crashed into the dining room, knocking into chairs and overturning tables, cutlery flying. Michael and his family fell back as Eric charged the windows, unloading another shot. Glass and ornate wooden framework exploded into the dark and he leapt through, stumbling onto the concrete at the petrol station.

He squinted at his car, then back at the desk clerk. The man's mouth hung open.

"Shit, I'm sorry, man." Eric fumbled for his wallet, ripped out some notes and threw them into the shattered glass inside the store. "Sorry." He leapt into the car and stomped on the pedal.

He drove until the station was distant, until he reached and passed the city limits, roaring into the sunset and then on into darkness. When the buildings stopped appearing he pulled into a truck stop beside the highway, high beams slaughtering shadows. A park bench and a grey rubbish bin stood in the light. He cut the engine but left the beams and radio on. The announcer was replaying an interview with Alfred Hitchcock. The old genius was explaining his famous actors and cattle quote.

Eric switched it off.

"What now?" he asked the dashboard.

No matter where he went, the *Rest* would find him. He'd open a door and it would be there, no way to know when or where. A new Oliver and the same old chef, expectant, determined.

"Why me?" They'd said something about wanting him so they could grow... but how exactly? Maybe it didn't matter – maybe what mattered was stopping them.

He tapped his fingers against the steering wheel. Without more information he wouldn't be much use. How did the chef know about his birth, how did she know to call him 'the boy who breathed disco'? Who'd be able to answer that?

Trash-Man maybe, but he was long gone, whoever he was.

What if...

Eric fired the engine. Time to travel back in time.

~~

The old guy was working the pokie machines, cup of gold coins in one hand and the other tapping the button for 'new spin'. The colourful glow from the screen was hypnotic and the super-cheerful music slicked the room with an insidious veneer of fun.

The old guy's rasping laugh was somewhere between gruff and chronic smoker. "Sure, I used to spin records here. That was before these pricks took over," he said, giving the poker machine a slap. "This joint used to be called *The Automatic*. Must be going back around thirty years. Man, we had some fun here. How'd you know?"

"My mother raised me here and the owner pointed you out. Says there's a framed newspaper article about you still up in the toilets."

"Right, that's the night Gwen Slater gave birth on the dance floor. Wild night."

"That was me," Eric said.

He blinked. "What?"

Eric pulled his licence from his pocket, handing it over. The ex-DJ set his cup of coins down. "My mother's Gwen," Eric said. "She said you held her hand."

"No shit?" He squinted at the card then gave it back with another smile. "This is pretty crazy, I gotta say. Nice to meet you, Eric. I'm Anthony."

"Can you remember much about that night? I'm trying to find someone who might have been there. I think she was a friend of Mum's."

"That's a big ask, lad."

"Well, you'd remember this particular lady. She was blonde and had wide-set blue eyes and she was pretty intense."

Anthony frowned, absently tapping the machine's buttons a few more times. "Maybe. I mean, lots of girls there that night and every night, but now that you mention it... there was a young lady who could have been her. Wild dancer."

"Really? Do you remember her name? Anything about her?"

"No. She was a regular that year but I can't say I ever saw her speak to anyone."

"What about that night? Was she there then?"

He shrugged. "Not sure, mate."

If the chef *had* been there, she'd aged remarkably well. "What about the music? Do you remember what you were playing when I was born? Mum thinks it's *I Will Survive* but Dad was sure it was *Lady Marmalade*. They used to argue about it."

"That I can definitely help you with," he said. "Your folks are both wrong, Eric. It was *Rikki Don't Lose that Number*, Steely Dan. 1974. Did better in the US than over here, but I always liked it. Put it on to slow the room down a bit, you know. You can't just play fast one after fast one, you know. It's a bit like being a conductor, except your orchestra is made up of every single body in the room."

Eric straightened. "Really? You're sure that was the one?" Hadn't Trash-Man been humming that song? And how could Mum and Dad *both* be wrong? A moment of high stress, definitely, but wouldn't the memory have been burnt in place?

"Yeah. I'll never forget that night." He slapped Eric's shoulder. "You've got a cool story to tell, that's for sure."

"Well, thanks for the help," Eric said as he stood, leaving the man to his machine.

He wove through the beeping, blinking poker machines and paused at the door, stepping aside for a pair of blue-rinse ladies to enter the venue. Either he'd gotten lucky on the way in, which had been a real risk, or he was too far from the city for the *Rest* to find him. No way to know without continuing to take risks.

He stepped out into midday sun.

Eric exhaled. Lucky. Or his guess was spot on; Disposable-Oliver and the chef couldn't reach him from so far away. He slowed on his way to the carpark... could he simply run then? Wasn't there a chance it'd never catch up with him? Or would he run forever and have to stay alone forever too, just in case? Live in a field beneath a tarp, never enter another building again.

It didn't seem like much of a life. And Michael, his wife and their little girls too; if there was a chance, Eric had to take a shot at freeing them. He still had Ben's shotgun in the car and maybe half a plan – but he needed a CD store first.

Just off Main Street there'd been a music shop when he was growing up. Would they have a copy of the song? Eric found his car and pulled onto one of the backstreets, crunching over autumn leaves as he closed in on *Purple Haze Records*. He parked out front.

Eric checked on the shotgun, hoping once again that it wouldn't be noticed when he was inside, then approached the glass. He allowed himself a split second of hesitation only before he pushed it open – and stepped into *The Gentleman's Rest*.

"God damn it."

Michael glanced up from where he sat alone at his usual table, his children playing quietly behind him. "It can find you just about anywhere."

Eric spun for the door – locked as ever. He strode to the window and pulled his gun... and stopped. Yes, he could probably bust his way free again, but what then? It was back to endless running, to fearing doors, and eventually, to an endless loneliness.

Something had to give.

"Are they in the kitchen?" he asked Michael.

"I think so." The man rose. "But you can't stop them that way."

"Let's find out," Eric said as he strode between the impeccably arranged tables. Silverware gleamed in the electric light as he passed, heading for the scent of mushroom soup. He kicked the kitchen doors open with a grunt.

A thin fellow with stringy blond hair stood over the soup, ladle in hand. The new Oliver? The man's head snapped around when he saw Eric and he raised a hand to point as Eric squeezed the trigger.

The shotgun blast tore the man's head from his shoulders.

It bounced across the bench top as the torso crumpled to the ground, ladle clattering across the floor.

Eric's stomach heaved but he leapt over the body, focusing on the cold room door. No sounds from beyond; where was the chef? He slapped a hand over the handle and ripped the door open.

Shelves of cold foodstuffs, vegetables and fruit, all chilled, stretched forward. A dull fluorescent light flickered overhead. A figure seemed to move beyond the edge of the light. Eric raised his gun and started forward.

The chef stood before a hunk of beef that hung from a meat hook.

She turned, her strange eyes sending their usual wave of nausea his way. "Eric, you cannot understand –"

He pumped the grip and fired again.

Blood exploded from her chest as the pellets tore into her torso. She was thrown to the floor, striking the meat on her way down. The hunk of beef swung, casting moving shadows as he stood over her. His arms were shaking but he kept a hold of himself somehow. The wide-set eyes turned to focus on him from where she lay in a pool of blood, her chef's whites stained red.

"We will not stop." Her voice was little more than a wheezing.

Eric swallowed as he lined up her head and pulled the trigger again.

The boom in the enclosed space tore into his ears; it didn't ease even after he'd stumbled out and into the kitchen, nor back into the dining area where he collapsed into a seat, gasping for air.

He was only vaguely aware of Michael standing before his girls.

"Where's your wife?" Eric asked. "You should get her; we can go now."

Uneven footsteps pounded along tiles, growing closer. Eric shot to his feet, gun held ready. One of the kitchen doors swung open, a bloody hand smearing the paintwork.

The chef stumbled free, leaning against the door. Her torso remained a gaping mess of torn flesh, pieces of shattered rib visible, but her head was what caused Eric to retch. It had somehow repaired itself – but not properly. One of her eyes sat down near the jaw bone, the other slid around near the opposite ear, like a half-melted frog. Her mouth was a jagged hole around fragments of teeth.

She spoke as she crept into the room, a single word only. The sound was little more than a grunt but when she lifted her hands, imploring as she repeated her attempt at speech, Eric shivered.

*Master.*

It was distorted, but she had cried for her master.

Eric spun, shotgun still in hand. Michael stood with one arm around each daughter, a sad smile on his face. "We will not stop, Eric."

His girls were fidgeting, their expressions unperturbed. Eric glanced at the Chef; she was leaning against the table nearest the kitchen, gripping her head as if dizzy.

"What is this?" Eric spat.

"We are lonely. It's been generations since we took on a new chef and nearly thirty years now since we found Oliver. You would be a most welcome introduction to the *Rest*. And more, you would be wonderful in growing our family."

"Family?" Eric lifted the weapon, his hands shaking once more. He gripped the shotgun harder, knuckles turning white. "What kind of monster would do *this* to his family? Look at your girls; they don't even know what's happening. And what about your wife? What have you done to her?" And that wasn't all. Hadn't there been another pair, glimpsed when *The Gentleman's Rest* appeared in his pantry? "And that couple, what about them?"

Michael did not answer, instead kneeling before his girls. "Why don't you play outside for a little? Not too far, mind."

They nodded and scurried through the front door, giggling and laughing.

When Michael rose, he still offered no answer.

"I have enough shells in this thing for you too," Eric told the man.

"Assuredly, but do you have enough for the next year?" he asked, his voice soft and reasonable. "Five years? Twenty, fifty? No matter how many times you shoot us, we will not stop."

Eric clenched his teeth.

"Please, set aside your gun. In time, Chef will reform properly and she can make us a nice meal. We can sit together and talk of the future. You will find much to appreciate within *The Gentleman's Rest*, Eric. There are richly appointed rooms above and much... enjoyment to be had from the hunt for new family members. I believe you would make a fine uncle. Yes, Uncle Eric, the words have a pleasant ring to them, don't you think?"

"This is insane. No!"

Michael took a single step forward, but raised his hands when Eric lifted the sawn-off. "Consider life beyond. You will never know a moment's peace. But if you stay here, where you belong..."

"I said no, you fucking freak – I didn't ask for this, do you understand?"

"Please. I will call Rikki and the girls in and you can get to know each other."

Eric opened his mouth but no words followed.

*Rikki.*

Her name was Rikki. Trash-Man had hummed *Rikki Don't Lose That Number* and Anthony claimed that was the song that played when Eric was born. It had to mean something! Rikki was the key, the wife was the key!

Michael's gentle expression switched to one of alarm – and it hit Eric. Up until that point, Michael had never used her name. As if he didn't want to draw attention to the fact. "Think about your future, Eric," Michael said, his concern evident.

And that was enough confirmation for Eric.

"I am," he said. Chef was now slumped against the table. The kitchen and storeroom were empty, he knew that. There didn't seem to be stairs leading up to another floor – which left the door indicating restrooms.

"No!" Michael roared as he leapt forward.

Eric swung the shotgun and fired, another reflex action.

The blast punched through the man's hips and Michael crashed to the floor.

Eric was already sprinting for the exit, shotgun in hand. It was now little more than a club, since he was out of shells. He looked back; Michael was dragging himself across the carpet, legs hanging uselessly behind him. Yet the man was snarling as he moved, unnaturally fast. Eric shouldered his way into a dim hall. No stairs in the darkness, but light crept from beneath the women's toilet door.

He burst inside. A heavy potted plant rested in the corner of the room. He dragged it screeching across the tiles to dump it before the door. How long it would last, he couldn't say but if it bought enough time... a long mirror ran opposite closed stalls.

His reflection showed a man with wild eyes, splattered blood covering his torn shirt and lost in dark hair. He hadn't shaved in days and his arms were twitching. The sawn-off shotgun was like a silent metal beast in his grip, the scent of gunpowder strong – a subtle reminder of what it could do, if unleashed once more. He looked like a man half a step removed from animal.

"You're here to end it, aren't you?"

Michael's wife stood at the far end of the row. She wore the same dark red dress from before, navy leggings beneath. She held nothing, not handbag nor weapon. Her eyes were red-rimmed, as though she'd been crying.

"How?" he asked.

Someone – or something – began pounding on the door.

She drew in a deep breath. "I'm linked to *The Gentleman's Rest*. If I die, it dies. You will be free, everyone will be."

He shook his head. Shooting someone that was hounding him, someone threatening to destroy his life, and as it turned out, someone who would not actually die as a result, that was one thing. What Rikki asked was something else entirely. "I can't do that to you. To your kids."

"They're safe; Michael has finally made a mistake."

"I don't understand."

"Then you will end up staying here forever, like the others."

The beating continued, yet it didn't seem that Michael would make much progress. Perhaps not being able to stand hampered his leverage.

"There has to be something else."

"There isn't, Eric." Fresh tears shone in her eyes.

He threw the shotgun aside. It slid beneath one of the stalls, cracking against the porcelain within. "No! I just have to think."

Michael was screaming – yet rage made his words incoherent.

Rikki approached, reaching out to take one of Eric's hands. She gave it a squeeze. "Listen. I know why he did it now, everything – especially our children. He tied me to the restaurant to possess me. The girls too; he knew I would never leave without my babies." She glanced away. "When we were first married... everything was different. Our first trip was by steam train. That's where he proposed. He was sweet, giddy, even. But it's like a decaying dream now. I've waited for courage for far too long."

Steam train? Just how old was she? "Then let me help you."

"You will, Eric. I need your promise first."

Outside, Michael's voice had risen to shrieking.

"Anything."

"Thank you." She withdrew a piece of folded paper, slipped it into his jeans pocket and stepped back. "I need a moment, Eric. Please make sure my husband does not find a way inside."

Eric frowned. "I will. But how are we going to escape?"

She moved back to the far stall and opened it, glancing back at him. "Just trust me a little longer, if you can."

He nodded.

Rikki closed the door. Eric started to pace. His pulse doubled as a different sense of wrongness filled the room, not the stomach-churning that Chef created, but a fear. It wasn't the thunder from the hall, lengthening gaps between thumping or the searing rasping voice to go with Michael's impotent fury – it came from the far end of the room.

"Rikki?"

He took a hesitant step forward.

"Are you sure I can't help?"

Still no answer issued from the final stall.

Eric quickened his stride. Beside him, the mirror seemed to bend. He spread his arms for balance as the floor rumbled. A wave of tiles rushed forward, tossing him to his knees. "Rikki?" He scrambled closer as plaster from the ceiling began to rain down. Dust puffed up and he strained for the door to her stall. His fingers gripped just enough to pull it open and he caught a glimpse of her feet, dangling above the toilet bowl...

And found himself sitting on plastic chair in a laundromat. Eric blinked, spinning in his seat. The place was empty, sagging music posters for long-finished tours resting above a row of white clothes dryers. The hum and spin of machines filled the room, the laughter of children drifted in from outside.

"Rikki?" he stood, but she was gone.

*The Gentleman's Rest* was gone too – and he knew why.

She had done what he could not, and freed him from the nightmare. Probably freed whatever remained of Oliver and Chef as well, though what that meant for those two, Eric couldn't guess. Would they even survive? And Michael. What of Rikki's husband? Did he disappear with the restaurant?

Eric slumped back into the chair, relief flooding through him, turning his limbs to water, a long sigh escaping.

The note!

He sat up, pulling the paper from his jeans to unfold it with trembling fingers.

*Please take care of Isabel and Rose.*

Eric glanced through the window to where two young girls danced and skipped along the footpath. He smiled. "I'll try."

# Somnus and the March Hare

Muted sunlight from dusty windows covered the piles, stacks, and lurking shapes of the op-shop's furniture. Michael placed the price tag, a square blot of yellowed paper, back onto varnished wood and rubbed his neck. He'd made a mistake. Letting it slip that he was recently widowed was definitely a mistake. The shop keeper, breathing heavy as he manoeuvred bedside tables, wore an expression of sympathy now. The man would probably want to give him a discount. Then it'd be extra guilt on top of the guilt of shopping in an op-shop, when he made enough not to. He should just walk down to Harvey Norman and go in there. Spend up like he was supposed to. Support the economy.

"Sir, would you like the hi-fi?" Puffing-man had a grey eyebrow raised. It got about halfway up his creased forehead without any trouble.

"Yeah. Yes please, I do."

"We can't deliver, just so you know."

"I've got a taxi outside."

"A taxi? He's been waiting for you all this time?"

Michael frowned. "I am paying him."

"Of course, I'm sorry, sir. Cash or card?"

He took out his wallet. "Cash."

At home he unpacked the various leads and cables, like a mess of emaciated snakes, and began untangling. It took him nearly an hour to sort everything and after various tests and a quick snack, he finally had a record player. In his shed, a box of records waited: those he'd purchased from shops like Batman Records and Collectors Corner as a teenager, before they disappeared, swallowed by the city's gluttony for Subway stores and designer labels. He hadn't been able to play them for years, not having a turntable—something that would have been his Christmas present.

When the needle touched down on *Kind of Blue*, he went right to *Flamenco Sketches* and simply sat at the kitchen table, only rising to reset the needle and cue it again when the song finished. It must have played half a dozen times when a whisper broke his trance-like state.

"Michael."

The voice cut over Miles' first solo—as if part of the track. Michael stood but the darkened room was empty and no-one's face was pressed against the window. The curtains. He shivered as he drew them across the glass, their hoops sliding, and reset the stylus. He waited, holding his breath.

The solo came and went and no-one spoke his name.

Michael frowned. Had he imagined the voice? Was he that tired? He moved the needle again and not until he'd played the song through twice did he stop, satisfied that there was no voice. His imagination, nothing more.

The rumble in his stomach was real and so he moved to the stove, shaking his head. He'd just got a pot boiling when the *Funeral March of a Marionette* rallied from the kitchen table. Between place settings arranged for two, the screen of his mobile glowed an insistent blue.

Work.

*No, Mr Roberts. Fix your damn computer yourself. This is the weekend.*

He slapped a second pot onto a hotplate and began to brown the meat, hacking at it with a wooden spoon. The grain rubbed against his skin and he imagined the sound of a pipe floating across a grassy hill. *Just what kind of wood are pipes made out of anyway? Wood like the spoon?* The muddy yellow pasta went in next, and when he was finally done, he took his half to the couch and began to eat without looking at the table.

~~

He woke with the scent of couch fabric pressed into his face, his shoulder stiff and mouth dry, sleep clogging his eyes. A pointless morning show prattled away; he'd left the television on again. *The door knocked?* No. Someone knocked on the door. He pulled himself up, rubbed his eyes and pushed a bag of clothes aside as he headed for the entryway. He'd slept on the couch again—a fitful hour, maybe less. His usual amount.

A Heart Foundation woman stood on his doorstep, silver tin and receipt book in hand. Dark hair, dark eyes, dark lashes, dark skin with white teeth above a dark blouse and a dark yellow skirt, just about dark-everything—even a single button on her blouse was dark.

"Sir? Good morning. My name is Ada and I'm collecting for the Heart Foundation."

When he didn't reply at once, her smile wavered. "Donations are tax-deductable."

"I'm sorry," he said, rubbing his eyes again. "I haven't been awake very long." She took her chance to launch into a speech, one he barely heard, but because she was pretty and he didn't want to seem like a mean-spirited jerk, he let her finish and when she paused for breath he said, "Let me get my wallet." He ducked inside, leaving her beaming on the step, and returned with a ten dollar note. Ada produced a pen from somewhere, writing out a receipt with perfect efficiency. He couldn't remember what he'd told her his name was.

"Thank you," she said, and walked back up his driveway, brushing at a cobweb that caught her where it stretched from car to front garden. He leaned against the doorframe and watched until she was out of sight, catching a glimpse of the banksia Sam had planted. He looked away, returning to the lounge where he collected his dishes and dropped them in the sink before moving on to the bathroom. By the time he'd showered and dressed, taking his time but not bothering to shave despite an itchy throat, he found six missed calls—all from Edward Roberts. Work. "Unlikely I'll make it in on time, Ed." The little hand resting on the ten confirmed it. Very late indeed. He shouldn't have stayed up all night, but he couldn't sleep in his bed.

In their bed.

Michael hit the green phone symbol twice to return the last missed call. He waited, pushing an apple across the kitchen countertop.

"Where the hell are you, Michael?" Edward Roberts was spitting.

"The kitchen," he said, but his voice was drowned out, Roberts was still going.

". . . because I've got a bunch of arseholes in the shop wanting to know when they can get their fucking Macs back and I can't make sense of your handwriting. What the fuck do you call those squiggles? And don't tell me you're taking the train again—it's quicker to drive, and you're late enough."

He waited for a slight pause. "Edward, I've just decided to quit. Thanks."

"So get in here and— You what?"

Michael ended the call and switched his phone off, tossing it onto the couch. "Wallet and keys," he mumbled.

~~

The collapse of REDGroup had taken with it Michael's ability to pay full retail for literature. He found instead a tiny spark in the form of discount books. Inside an Angus and Robertson, its staff frowning through their customer-service smiles, he flipped through a *Lord of the Rings* knock-off, then a little of a Caroline Graham Inspector Barnaby novel, but put them both down when he saw a picture book lying on a pile of boxes. An illustrated *Alice's Adventures in Wonderland,* it looked like the very same children's book he'd owned as a kid. "It is," he murmured when he picked it up. Not much text and large, brightly coloured pictures. At least, bright until he reached the Tea Party. It was shaded a deep red and black, with patches of orange and brown, just as he remembered it. The characters were all there, including a very mangy March Hare crouching atop the table, a purple tea cup in hand and yellow eyes lidded. It was thin, sickly-looking, but very real. More vivid than he recalled. Several whiskers were missing and it wore no jacket or hat, as he'd seen in other representations.

"Nice detail," he murmured, and stroked the Hare.

His fingers brushed fur and he blinked as the March Hare leapt into his palm, nearly slipping out, tea cup still in hand. A tuft of fur floated to the ground. The Hare blinked up at him, nose twitching. He could almost taste the animal through his gaping mouth. The March Hare pointed outside, jabbing its paw at the air. Michael complied, cupping his hands and stumbling out, no doubt looking like a nutjob, hunched over and unshaven, his clothes rumpled. No-one was going to ask him if he needed any assistance today.

Cold air in the busy street told him his eyes were comically wide—looks from passing people confirmed it and he flinched whenever the Hare moved. A nearby park drew him in, where he ran to a green bench in an out of the way corner and sat, glancing at the trees before opening his hand.

"Stop shaking, will you," the Hare demanded. Its small eyes rolled and the nose twitched when Michael made a squeaking sound. "That the best you can do?"

"No, no, I can talk."

"Wonderful. But you're in trouble and you don't know it, do you, Michael? Now take me back to the suburbs, to your house."

He stood and placed the March Hare into his pocket, nearly giggling when it wriggled around and tickled him. "I must be hysterical," he said. To the Hare he apologised. "We have to take the train."

"Why is that?" the voice was muffled.

"Because we have to . . ." he didn't continue, and walked back to the train station, fortunate that his arrival coincided with the departure of his line. The March Hare was quite still until over an hour later, when Michael dashed up his driveway and entered the house, waving a postman away as he did so. The man knocked twice but Michael ignored him. Instead he set the March Hare on the kitchen bench and watched it shed fur as it slapped on the bottom of its tea cup, head tilted back, a continuous flow of brown liquid pouring out. It smelled like bourbon and it went on for some time.

"What should I call you?" he finally asked.

"March Hare is fine." The small animal wiped its mouth.

He took a breath. "Okay."

The March Hare continued to drink, ribcage visible through the mottled fur that covered its breast. Finally the creature stopped. "All right, where is your bookcase?"

"In the study."

"Well?"

"Well, what?"

"You have to carry me, Michael."

"Why are we going to the bookcase?" Michael held out his hand, which the Hare leapt onto. The little pads were smooth and cold on his palm, reminding him this all was real. On the train, when it didn't move or talk, he'd actually half-convinced himself he'd imagined the hare, suffering some sort of sleep deprivation-induced hallucination. "Did you want to read a book?" he asked, coming to a halt before the bookcase. One of Sam's bookmarks was sticking out of *Written on the Body* by Jeanette Winterson, where it was wedged between a few of his wife's other books on one side, and his own on the other. Too many had unbroken spines.

"Where is your mythology section, then?"

"Section? This isn't a library."

"Fairy tales?"

"Why?"

"Because you need sleep and I know someone who might help, depending on the price."

"You're going to hand me over to Sleeping Beauty, I

suppose?"

The rabbit sighed. "No, you half-wit. The Roman God of Sleep, Somnus. Now hush. Ah, there, he's mentioned in that one, open it up—the one with the green stripe on the cover. Page seventy-eight, open it up."

Michael did so, unable to hold back a frown when instructed by a royal wave of the purple cup, which was now empty, to place the Hare onto the page. "Here, he's in here somewhere. Line twelve, word six, ah-ha. You wait here for a while." The March Hare began burrowing into the pages, sending shredded paper flying. The Hare was muttering about how much easier it was with pictures and the confetti kept flying until the animal was out of sight. When it stopped, Michael peered into an empty hole.

"March Hare? Where are you, you bossy little bastard?"

When no voice was forthcoming, Michael went back to the kitchen and took a long drink of water. Maybe he should call someone and tell them about the March Hare. A doctor? One of his friends? Family? He'd sound like a lunatic, but at least he could talk to them without being insulted. They'd laugh, and then there'd be worried whispers and maybe some sort of meeting. And it would all end with sedation and commitment forms signed by his well-meaning loved ones, but they would try to understand at least. He found his mobile and let his thumb hover over the power button, closing his eyes.

No. Not worth bothering them. Not so soon after the accident.

Checking on the book, which was still the proud owner of a fair-sized hole, and finding neither the mythical Somnus nor a curt rabbit, he returned to his lounge and flicked the television on. Greeted with pointless life insurance ads, he turned it off, threw *Flamenco Sketches* back on the turntable, and made himself a sandwich, careful not to use the out-of-date ham Sam had been saving for a barbeque.

He'd just finished eating, wiping crumbs from the bench with his arm, when the revving of a neighbour's motorbike cut through the music. Michael fought the urge to shout at the man, but it served to remind him of the postman, so he let it go. A rectangular box sat on his doormat, half-covering the word *Welcome*. From Brisbane, New Farm—a salvage job on a hard drive.

Michael placed the package on the kitchen table and rummaged around for his gear, taking everything into the study. Might as well wait and work at the same time. There was no way to know how long the crazy rabbit would be gone, or even if it would return.

The client's hard drive was a mess. Michael's mouse clicks grew further and further apart. His attention was drawn to the book. The March Hare was vague. How long did it consider a "while" to be? Was it a "while" like the way it took an hour for the train to get in to the city, or was it more like a day or two, the way it took a "while" for interstate mail to arrive? He had no idea of its concept of time, let alone how it'd fallen out of the children's picture book in the first place. And why was it so convinced he needed sleep? He should have purchased the book.

The computer pinged and he jumped. A dialog box flashed on-screen, a winking March Hare placed in the corner. It instructed him only to *Go to bed*.

Michael had to laugh. "What?"

The dialog box changed. *Just do it, Michael.*

"You want me to go to sleep?" Being bossed around was starting to wear thin. "Listen, March Hare, I guess you're trying to help, but I'm not tired. And I can't sleep anyway. I haven't been able to sleep for a week."

The image frowned. *I know that. Just do as I say, Somnus is waiting. Go and make a deal with him. It was very hard to get him here, don't waste it.*

"Heavy sleeper, is he?"

The screen went black. Michael nudged the mouse but the computer didn't respond so he moved down his hall, taking a deep breath. It had grown somewhat dark for midday and when he entered the room, it was dim as if the sun had been blocked by heavy curtains—which it had. Only they weren't his curtains. Thick drapes of light-swallowing velvet lined the room. The rustle of feathers came from the bed, which was no longer his bed, but a grand four-poster complete with a pale young man with marble-Roman features, reclining against massive black cushions. He was naked from the waist up but lay beneath blankets formed from thousands of black feathers.

*Sit with me.* Somnus' eyes were closed but his head followed Michael as he crept forward, a shaking hand extended to touch the bed.

"Oh god," he said. "This is real too."

*Of course. Now sit with me and we will discuss the terms of our deal.* Somnus patted the bed beside him.

Michael hesitated.

*Remove your shoes and clothes, Michael,* Somnus soothed him.

He did as commanded, undressing without shame, and sat on the end of the bed, finding the feathers to be soft, their quills missing. Something held him back, despite the warm darkness and the calm coming from the serene Somnus.

*You know you will have to lie down to sleep.*

"I do," Michael whispered. "You mentioned terms?"

*As the God of Sleep, I can grant rest such as your body and soul will never again experience, though that is a price you cannot afford. Instead, I am willing to exchange your sleep for that of another human's.*

"Permanently?"

*Certainly not.*

"So I have to give up a night's sleep? But I'm barely sleeping an hour a night."

*There are those willing to trade their peaceful sleep for such a night as you describe.*

Michael nodded. "What do I need to do?"

Somnus' eyes opened and blazed with a darkness that spread out from his face, filling Michael's bedroom. His voice whispered beyond the ink. *Simply lie down beside me and you will sleep.*

Michael crawled forward and stretched out on his back. Soft hands pulled the feathers over him and he tried to speak, but the black was seeping into his mind. It tickled his ears and nose. He took a deep breath, sucking it in.

~~

Something loud woke him. A crash and a shout, followed by footsteps. He lay still a moment but there was only a neighbour's lawn-mower, toiling away. A dream. He stretched on the sheets, searching for cool spots. He could smell Sam beside him and glanced at the clock, thinking it was too early for some inconsiderate chump to be mowing. Living in the suburbs had its price.

*Somnus!* He sat up, but his bed was just an ordinary king-sized bed. An empty king-sized bed. Sam was still gone. His curtains were tan once more and there was not a single feather in the room. But he was refreshed. It was the best sleep he'd had in a week. In a year. Whose night of sleep had he taken, and what had they done with his night of wakefulness? Something criminal? Michael got out of bed and stumbled into the study, where the book lay open. He ran his hand over the hole's rough edges, exhaling. In the kitchen, he half-expected to find the March Hare waiting for him, but there was no small creature on the bench, purple teacup of bourbon in hand. Or paw.

But there was a souped-up Holden in his lounge room.

Covered by the shattered remnants of his front wall, window and a cabinet, it had completely crushed the couch—his customary sleeping place since Sam's accident. The blue car was empty but footprints were visible in the carpet of plaster. They led out to the garden. Whoever crashed into his house was gone. Dust motes swirled in the early morning light, they looked joyful.

And he'd slept through it, from the safety of his bedroom. The March Hare saved his life. The damn creature lent him to the God of Sleep and it saved his life. He fell back against the kitchen bench, knocking something over. Sirens began to wail and from next door, voices called out, but he ignored them, instead crouching to pick up a picture frame, the object he'd knocked down. It was broken but the photo rested face up, expectant. He and Sam were sitting in a café, the sun warming her hair. She was smiling at him as he held his birthday present, a vinyl copy of *Kind of Blue.*

Michael placed the photo on the bench. For a week he hadn't been able to look at it, but now he couldn't turn away. He was shuddering, and the salt of his tears burned lips and tongue. He heaved a sob and it was as if a black mass of poison burst out of him.

He blinked.

Splattered across the bench, hissing and eating into its surface, was what looked like tar. Spots of it sizzled on the fruit bowl and floor, and the edges of the photograph were already curling. Michael snatched it up and rinsed it under the sink, washing his mouth out too, when the burning continued.

When he straightened his chest muscles and shoulders were loose. The sound of birdsong drifted in, quieter but stronger than the sirens. It was a light sound, nimble, and he almost smiled. A weight that seemed natural for such a long time was gone, banished. He stood back and let the bench deteriorate, holding the photo to his chest as tears blurred the edges of the room.

# Red Madam

Eddie tossed the death-sentence in a letter onto his desk, scratching at the stubble on his throat. The words were fine. Eloquent even. What didn't make sense was the fact that someone had been stupid enough to commit them to paper in the first place.

The thin whistle of an old hybrid train pierced the red walls of his office, slicing through despite the lack of a window. He snorted as he leant back in the creaking chair. Who needed a view? Nothing out there but grey skies and the dark neons of a decaying city, anyway.

He squashed his cigarette into the letter, thumping the embers with the heel of his hand.

*This bloody thing will get me killed.* And maybe that didn't matter?

Better sooner rather than later, perhaps.

High heels clacked along a stone floor, approaching swiftly. He slid the letter into a desk drawer. Through frosted glass in the door he marked her shape approaching. Eddie pulled off his hat. "Damn it." His coat dripped from a peg by the door. Too bad if she noticed; she probably already knew what he'd done.

Madam Jessica entered without knocking. She stood wrapped in a dark gown such as he'd never seen on her – the garment could have been soot. It matched her eyes; both cold as fossils.

"You've been out again. Alone. Without me." The frown was clear in her voice, as though the words had an unpleasant aftertaste. Her face remained smooth.

"I know what 'alone' means, Madam."

Now her eyes narrowed. "Don't do that, Eddie. You're a man, not a priest. Respect, Eddie. Respect."

"I respect you, Madam." He offered her a cigarette.

"Don't be ridiculous." She sat across from him, barely denting the leather back. The old chair was a throne when she occupied it.

Madam Jessica placed a small, egg-shaped recorder on the desk between them and pressed a button. A tiny blue light flicked on. "Where did you go, Eddie?"

Not point lying; not that anyone ever did. "To the waterfront."

She smiled, even as she shook her head. "Why did you go to the waterfront without me?"

"I was meeting a friend."

She raised a feathery eyebrow. "Who?"

"Tommy."

"The rebel."

"The factory worker. I was playing poker."

She leant forward, just enough pale cleavage to draw his eye. He looked away. Bad idea, Eddie. Good way to get yourself killed, especially if someone else sees you doing that.

"Eddie, what makes you think I'd believe that? A cop playing an innocent game of poker with a rebel?"

He rubbed his jaw. What would happen if he 'accidently' broke the recorder? Jessica's lips thinned into a line and she placed a manicured hand on the table, the crimson-painted nails a match for his walls. "Answer my question, Eddie. Don't make me use the Pulse."

Eddie leant back. When a Madam used the Pulse Ring

on a man, whoever he was, he squirmed. If he had to describe it, having burning sand poured into his lungs would have come close. Not that he'd felt it in years, didn't want to feel it again either. And not from Jessica.

She pounded the desk. "Well?"

*I should have burnt this.* Eddie opened the drawer and handed her the letter.

~~

She put the paper down, crinkling the edges. Her face was set like bleached concrete and a vein pulsed in her neck. Sweat should have been tearing a path down his back but he was ... empty. *Too tired to be afraid, Eddie?*

Jessica pressed the button again and the light on the recorder died. "By law I should kill you right now, Eddie, just for having that." She whispered, but it didn't mask the fury of her words.

He shrugged. "But you won't, will you, Madam?"

She slapped him. "You're not untouchable, Eddie. Anyone but me, *anyone*, and you'd be dead right now." She snatched the letter and recorder as she stood. "You're going to the waterfront tonight and you're going to kill Tommy. Since he was stupid enough to write this, he will take your punishment."

Eddie blinked, raising a hand to a cheek. He shook his head. "What if the other Madams –"

"They won't. You're damn lucky, Eddie. You kill Tommy and I pretend you never had the letter." Her voice softened a fraction as she turned to leave. "Take it or leave it."

She closed the door before he could reply.

~~

Eddie splashed through the dark, lamp-lit streets. His hat's brim funnelled water onto the shoulders of a waxed trench coat. Madam Anna, his Night Madam, strode beside him, her boots smacking against wet concrete. He'd already offered his coat, but her war-suit, complete with hood and gloves, was water-resistant. Crafted by prisoners in underground labs, it was impervious to elements and most forms of violence. Compared to his pitiful body armour, it was a queen's garment. *They ought to make me something like that. I'm the one running around doing their bloody dirty work.*

Anna slapped his arm. "Look!"

Eddie pulled his gun. A shadow moved across an intersection. It was big. Fast. "Curfew breaker?" He knew he was wrong even as he spoke.

"No. It's a mutant."

"In the city?" Eddie strained his eyes, trying to pierce heavy rain where it pummelled the glistening streets. It was like an ever-changing screen. Without the lights there'd be nothing but black on black. The shape moved again, slipping between the jagged fountain and the glow from an IVF Centre. "The army boys usually aren't this lax, Madam Anna."

She glanced at him. "The Mother has cut funding to the Border Forces."

He turned a half-arc, barrel trained on the patches of darkness between pale float-lamps. "Is that wise? Who's going to protect the civilians?"

Anna sneered. "What would a man know, Edward? Just a week ago a soldier turned his rifle on a Madam. He never got to fire, of course, the chip terminated him in time, but it just goes to show how untrustworthy you lot are, even in this day and age." She waved a hand. "And Officers like you can protect the precious civilians. Now hurry up and take me to this warehouse. I'm tired of the rain."

*Not my place to voice an opinion.*

Even so, the Mother was making a mistake. What lurked beyond the city's perimeter was not pretty. He'd spent his youth on the border and some of the things he'd killed, especially near the dead ocean... small mercy that he'd only seen half of them. Just the flash of guns in the black and the unsteady glow of old float-lamps jammed in his memory.

He moved on, keeping his weapon out. He'd have to oil it later, but there was no way he was putting it away, not with a mutant running around the city. And it wouldn't be the only one.

Cutting through a stinking alley, he led his warden to the waterfront and stopped before a modest, red warehouse. "This is it, Madam Anna." A faded AirForce Wing was emblazoned upon the rolling doors. Light poured from high windows and the clanging of metal slamming against metal, of screeching drills and shouted orders, slipped into the street.

"Let's get this over with." Anna punched a code into the security panel. The door slid open and she beckoned for Eddie to follow. The interior of the warehouse was blessedly dry. Between pauses in the clamour, rain hammered against the roof, as though trying to force a way inside. Men in overalls rushed between hulking plane-parts for the Women's AirForce, carrying sheets of hyper-carbon and large rivet guns. The workmen ignored them, but a woman in a work-suit marched over and asked that they state their purpose.

"I see," she said after a moment's conference with Anna. "This way, Madam."

He trailed the two women to the back row. A group of factory hands sat on crates, eyes fixed on a card game. Their faces were smudged with grease and several bore burn-scars along their arms. *Courtesy of engine faults too messy for a woman to fix, no doubt.*

Tommy put his cards down when he saw Eddie, before standing and offering a deep bow to the two women. "Good Evening, Madams."

Madam Anna's gaze was dispassionate. "You are Tommy Geran?"

"Yes."

"Then you are charged with conspiring against the Mother. A treasonous letter in your handwriting has been recovered. You are a threat to the Peace and will be punished. Eddie?"

Eddie raised his gun. The barrel was almost as thick as his arm.

The factory workers threw their cards down with shouts, backing up against the wall. Tommy fell to his knees, his eyes owl-wide. "Eddie, please! We're family."

"Sorry."

Eddie braced his shoulder and pulled the trigger.

The shot ripped through the warehouse with a flash and an echo, punching a hole in Tommy's chest the size of his skull.

Anna sniffed. "I think we're done here."

~~

Eddie paced his red apartment. Painfully dull. Red walls, red ceiling, red curtains and thin, red carpet. He dragged a chair up to the window. In the tight courtyard below, a pot plant and headstone he'd fashioned for his old Labrador caught the rising sun.

More red.

Tommy's eyes. *They'd been so damn wide.*

Eddie lit a smoke. Maybe the women painted every male building red, not for identification, but to hide the bloodstains. His cousin's last words echoed, but mostly there was the letter. Some of the things it had said, about how the male side of humanity was under threat, how it was slowly being bred out of existence on earth, had to be true. *Look at how many IVF centres they have now. And that sperm-drive. It went on for months. They outnumber us five to one.* Maybe he hadn't cared before, but it was clear now – now when he didn't need to care.

He finished his cigarette and went to the bathroom to shave. The Madams didn't like beards. Barbarians wore beards, they said. "And slaves wear nothing on their faces," he muttered.

"Did you say something, Eddie?" The wall muffled Madam Jessica's voice. "Have you forgiven me? I was in a bad mood yesterday. You worried me."

Eddie smiled. Would she ever finish dressing? "It's nothing, Madam. But you are forgiven."

She came to stand behind him. In the mirror, she tied up waves of autumn hair, revealing the china-doll skin of her neck and shoulders. "You said something. I heard you. Are you worried about Anna? She didn't see me; she never does. Or maybe it's what was inside the letter? It's not that cut-and-dried, you know. We'd never remove the entire male line. We need you, don't forget that."

He sighed as he put away the laser-blade. "Just talking to myself. How do I look?"

"Good enough." She smiled. "I have something special planned for today, I thought you'd like to –" Jessica stopped. "Eddie, what's wrong?"

"I don't –" He staggered, catching the doorframe. The room spun. His gut churned, as though someone had flicked the switch on a blender. The pain drove him to one knee and he gasped.

Jessica put a hand on his shoulder then withdrew it. "Eddie, where does it hurt?"

"My stomach." He ground out the words from between clenched teeth. Like forcing them up a cliff. *God, not again, not so soon.*

"I'll get a doctor."

Eddie shook his head. "Don't bother." He sucked in air. "I'm all right now. It's passing."

Jessica waited, her brow creased. Eddie hauled himself to his feet and after another lungful of air, stumbled past her and into the hall, where he strapped on his gun and slid an arm into his coat.

Her voice stopped him. "Why don't you see a doctor? You've been having these fits for weeks."

He didn't turn, only continued dressing. "I've already been."

Jessica moved to his side. "And?"

Eddie felt his jaw tighten. "There's no beds for my kind,

Madam."

A shadow passed over her lovely face. "What is it? What do you have?"

He shrugged. "Some sort of new cancer. But there's no surprise there, there's a new one every week thanks to the pollution – it's in everything. Everyone knows it and no-one acts." He opened the door and a blast of winter air tugged at his coat. "We'd better get to the office before someone misses us."

~~

Eddie slumped in his seat, lit another cigarette and looked over his last report. Nestled within the digital shards were the careful lies he'd built around Tommy's futile rebellion. Once it was signed he could hand it over to Jessica and then, as his Day Madam, she would pass it on to the Mother's Library. It seemed good enough to fool the others. *Too bad if it isn't. Won't matter soon.* He tapped his Ink-less on the desk as he read it one last time.

"Have you thought about what we discussed last night, Eddie?"

He didn't look up. "No."

Jessica leant across the table. "If you'd agree to the implant you wouldn't have to risk your life every day. You could live without fear. We could stop hiding."

Eddie put down the report. "I'd be an even bigger slave than I am now. If I let them put the *Omega* in my brain then I might as well be dead."

"But you'll die!" Jessica lowered her voice. "Eddie, if you take the implant, you'll qualify for treatment." She caught his arm and shook him. "Listen to me. If you cared for me you'd –"

"No, Madam. If *you* cared for *me* you'd remove the chip. You'd free me." As soon as the words tumbled forth, a weight lifted. For months now, even after he found out about the cancer, he'd been meaning to ask her. And it wasn't fair, to expect her to risk her own life with such a request, but just once – damn it, once – he wanted to feel total free will. The kind his forefathers experienced.

Her eyes glistened and her fingers dug into his flesh. "I can't."

"Don't lie."

"It wouldn't make any difference if I did."

"Not if we faked my death. Then they wouldn't investigate the removal of the chip."

"We'd never pull it off. Even if we did, you'd need treatment for the cancer, and there's something else, Eddie, there's –"

He cut her off. "Forget the cancer. I want to be free, Madam. Terminal illness or not."

"You'd choose death over me?"

Eddie said nothing and Jessica drew back, hurt bright in her eyes. The silence in the room was worse than the old graveyard he'd snuck into beneath the city as a child. At least there he'd imagined the sound of ghosts, the room seemed stuffed with them now. Everything he wanted to explain, his anger, his pain and his regret, his love; ghosts all if he left them unsaid.

*But what if she doesn't understand?*

Finally Jessica rose and came to stand behind him, waving him down as he sought to face her. Her voice was robotically toneless. "Eddie, give me your ear. Don't argue, just do as I say."

He complied, tilting his head to one side. He saw her raise the Pulse Ring. "You don't know what this means to me, Madam," he whispered.

"This will hurt, Eddie." She placed the Ring to his ear.

Pain shot down his neck and into his spine. The shockwaves looped and he clenched his jaw – but it was over so fast. It still left him breathing hard and blood trickled from his ear in a trail to his collar, but he didn't wipe it away.

Jessica placed a small, blood-covered *Alpha*-chip in his palm.

"How did you –"

Madam Anna burst into the room, flanked by a pair of Officers from another precinct.

"Arrest that man for treason." She spat the order.

"What is this?" Jessica demanded. She intercepted the men and glared at the other Madam. "You can't just accuse an Officer without proof, Anna."

"I have proof. I collected the mind of Tommy Geran for research and found something incriminating in his memories."

Even in his state of joy, Eddie cursed himself for a fool. With one hand he clutched the chip and with the other, he reached for his gun. Slowly. He should have gone for a headshot that night, but the guy was family. *Uncle Phillip wouldn't have wanted his only son mutilated.* Now it was Eddie's turn. *Die fighting now or die of cancer later.*

"Jessica, down!" He drew and fired, quicker than he'd ever moved.

The blast caught Anna in the neck, splattering blood

across the stunned faces of her guards.

Jessica screamed a warning, her eyes wide as she called for him.

But there was no need.

Having just witnessed the impossible, a man firing upon a woman, the Officers were far too slow. Two more shots echoed in the red room and both men hit the floor, one twitching, the other still.

Eddie slumped back in his chair, dazed. *What was happening?* It wasn't right, having to kill the men, but there'd been no other way. "Jessica?" The room was darkening, crimson walls turning to black as he frowned at the ceiling. *Who got me? I didn't feel it. Hell, I didn't even see it.*

Jessica's body pressed against him and he fumbled for her hand, slipping the *Alpha* into her palm. He dropped the gun, mumbling a curse. Why had she become little more than a silhouette? "I got them all. Damn it, what's wrong with me? Jessica?"

"I know you did, Eddie, I know you did." She stroked his hair.

~~

"It was the chip, Eddie." Jessica closed her eyes. A hole was growing in her heart, spreading wider and wider, a new abyss that she knew she'd never fill. "I couldn't take it out – not without it killing you. I tried to tell you, you stubborn fool."

He didn't reply.

Jessica took a deep breath, squeezing his fingers. Eddie sat in the chair, body free of wounds, eyes blank. His gun lay smoking by his boot.

*Did he hear me?* Jessica looked over at the Night Madam. Anna's head rested several feet from her body. Blood still pumped from the neck arteries, seeping under the door. There wasn't much time; others would already be on closing in on the station. If she was going to protect his memory, it had to be now. Jessica turned back to Eddie and kissed his cheek before lifting his gun.

So heavy. The metal singed her hand, but she placed the barrel against Eddie's temple and turned her face to the wall, closing her eyes and pulling the trigger.

Steelhand

Oscar let his end of the railway sleeper thump into the frost-bitten ground. He paused, the clink of hammers and shouts from the other workman washing over him as he stared up beyond the hill to the steel spires. They were like blackened fangs thrust into the wintry sky. Nothing like the belching spires and neat, sooted brickwork of the city, no.

These were different.

Real *feats of engineering*. Dark magic, old gaffers claimed and Oscar had always laughed at them as they spat their murky tobacco. But today, the forest of steel pumped steam into the air – even from a distance, down here where the rail would one day pass – and he couldn't stop a shiver.

"There's a hidden castle in there, you know," Nicholas sniffed from where he still held his end of the squared lumber. "And a sleeping princess, most beautiful woman ever. Hair soft as midnight. Princess Charlotte."

Oscar raised an eyebrow. He'd heard similar stories himself. "You've been listening to those old codgers?"

Nicholas barked a short laugh, air steaming from his mouth. "I'm not the one who stopped to stare, am I?"

"I've never seen it."

"Well now you have." He patted the sleeper. "Come on, we've got a lot more of these bastards yet."

Oscar hesitated; a blue light seemed to stir within one of the spires.

"What now?" Nicholas said.

The light faded. "I thought I saw something..." Oscar

shrugged, then bent to lift his end, the mechanical hand within his glove gripping far more easily than his real hand, and they resumed their trek to the front of the line.

"She's supposed to have been sealed in there for a hundred years. Some alchemist put her to sleep, seeing as she wouldn't have him for a husband."

"That so?"

"It is. They say the king refused the alchemist; now she and the rest of the castle-folk are stuck there, waiting for someone to rescue her while the alchemist roams the halls like a corpse, pining for the woman who spurned him."

Oscar shook his head. "You're a rotten liar, Nicholas."

"Just repeating what I heard."

"Well, save it. It's an old story and it doesn't even make sense. Why would he put her to sleep? I don't think she'll change her mind when she wakes."

He grinned. "Nor do I, but I find it pretty amusing that you're giving it so much consideration. I thought I was a 'rotten liar'."

"You are," Oscar snapped back as they manoeuvred the piece of timber into place at the end of the line, dropping it into the hole dug into the near-frozen earth. Yet he couldn't prevent himself looking to the spires once more as they returned to the pile of lumber.

~~

*Oscar!*

A woman's sweet voice called to him.

*Oscar, please – I need your help; I've been trying to reach you. You can hear me, can't you?*

Oscar woke to the pale light of pre-dawn where it slipped between the curtains like ghostly fingers across his face, remnants of a dream spilling onto his lumpy pillow. He'd been charging through the halls of a darkened castle, calling for the princess to awaken.

He sat up, a frown on his face. Had he truly heard the woman's voice?

Or was it just another whisper from the dream?

Across the city, a steam train sounded its mournful horn as it pulled into the station. *Time to get on with the day.* If he tarried he'd be late and the chief engineer was tediously humourless when it came to such things. Oscar threw his blankets aside and dressed, sure to pull his gloves on, concealing the shame of his one mechanical hand. He took a bite from a wrinkled apple as he threw on his coat and stepped onto a frosty street.

Cold air bit into his cheeks as he walked. People were already about, workmen like he, hunched into their coats as they hurried along the dim streets. A steam-cart rattled up the street – within, a woman wearing a spotless white dress laughed as it passed. Above the rows of black-tiled rooves were the great, beast-like towers of Factory Row. Their black maws belched a steady stream of smoke and ash into the sky.

*Oscar, you must answer me. He's nearly figured it out.*

He stopped. Now *that* had been no dream. The woman's voice was clear as a silver bell. He glanced around the quiet buildings, some with smoke rising from their own chimneys, but no-one was about. Oscar stepped into an alley. "Hello?" He kept his voice low.

*You* do *hear me!*

"I do, Lady."

*My name is Charlotte. You must save me. Come to the forest of spires – it must be today.*

"Princess Charlotte? From the old stories?"

*Yes.*

He swallowed. That wasn't possible, surely? It was the stuff of fairy tale and legend. Or madness, more likely.

*You are not mad, Oscar. I know you saw my sign, the flicker of blue light in the forest. Fate has chosen you to save me.*

"Fate?" Could he really leave today? What would Nicholas say? And the engineer – the line had to be completed before the winter snows and they were behind schedule. People depended on him. The rail would increase trade. Better food would become available.

*I'm depending on you too, Oscar. In one hundred years no-one has heard me. Please.*

And yet, wouldn't finishing the rail simply line the pockets of the rich lords and ladies who owned it? Oscar took a breath. *If I save Charlotte maybe she'll see me as a hero, instead of a flawed man.* Steelhand, other women had spat, when they spurned him. "Where are you?"

*In the castle at the centre of the steel spires. But you must bring three items if you are to succeed.*

"I have little money, My Lady."

*A rusted axe, a toy soldier crafted of wood and a single lemon, that is all. Hurry, Oscar. Silas has nearly discovered the final ingredient in his latest concoction. You must stop him. I was never supposed to sleep so long but he's found a way to change everything now. If he uses it I won't be able to refuse him. Please come swiftly.* She was almost babbling, her words tumbling over one another.

"Who is Silas? The Alchemist?" He waited but she did

not answer. "Princess Charlotte?"

Oscar turned and ran from the alley.

~~

He stood at the bottom of the hill before towering rows of steel. Each spire thrust up from the cold ground like an unyielding tree. Many were pitted with age, blackened or worn from wind and weather but the grey wall did not appear weak. Some spires were so tall and thick they completely blocked the sun, others were mere saplings, but all were jammed together so that surely no path between them existed.

Oscar hefted his father's old axe with a doubtful glance at the rust-covered blade. In a simple sack slung across his chest was a bright yellow lemon, and toy soldier with a blue uniform who carried a rifle and bayonet and determined expression. He'd bartered hard for the little fellow.

"I hope you're right about everything, Lady Charlotte," he said as he strode forward. He could not manage more than a few paces into the spires before the way was blocked by a thicket of steel saplings, each no broader than his thigh. He levelled a kick at one and a clang followed, shockwaves riding up his leg. The sapling hadn't budged.

*Axe it is then.*

Oscar took a breath and swung. The blade crashed into the sapling, cleaving it in two with a puff of rust and sparks. The top half clanged against the other spires as it fell and he leapt back. He scratched his head. "Sorry I doubted you, Lady."

He swung the axe again, felling another, then a third and

fourth until he had an opening he could squeeze through. A narrow clearing lined by heavier, broader steel trees waited, grown so tight that only a feeble shaft of sunlight entered. Here the thrumming of engines, deep below, grew stronger. A burst of steam escaped a hole in a tree branch, high above.

"More of you, I see." Oscar hacked into the thickest trunk, chopping and chopping with the rusted axe until he was covered in sweat. When he paused for breath, the air no longer chilled him – had it grown warmer? The engines were rumbling now, ground trembling, but he kept on until he'd cut a rough tunnel through the giant spire.

More trees beyond, but the hint of a path too. He slumped against the broad trunk a moment, breathing hard.

Behind him, the way out was closed.

He straightened. "How..." The saplings had grown back. More of the Alchemist's foul magic? He growled as he stood, scrambling through the opening he'd cut, then charged on, hacking and slashing with the rusted axe, sparks flying as he leaped over the debris.

As the day wore on his muscles grew weary but still he fought the machines until, as darkness started to fall across the forest, he stumbled free. An ancient castle loomed before him, its arched windows all dark and its parapets empty of defenders. No pennant flew from the peaked towers.

The door was made of heavy wood, reinforced with iron bands. Before the entry sat a swan-shaped fountain, which he approached with careful steps. No strange blue light appeared, no sounds, no people issued forth. Where was Princess Charlotte, where was Silas the Alchemist? The tallest tower? Doubt grew and even though he didn't want to, he thought of his steel hand. Even if he found a way inside, even if he saved her, would she snicker at him? She was noble-born after all and he was a lowly labourer.

"Get a grip, Oscar," he told himself. "She said Fate chose you."

Water bubbled in the fountain; it caught the last of the dying light and he knelt to drink. Cool and sweet, it coursed through his veins and he stood with a gasp. His fatigue was gone! Oscar drank his fill and a kind presence washed over him, it was as if he'd been blessed.

"Lady Charlotte, is that you?"

*Yes. Hurry, Oscar.* Desperation bled through her voice. *Silas has started the potion! I feel so weak. I cannot fight the dream much longer.*

"I'm coming." Oscar ran to examine the gate. The wood was chill beneath his palm yet it did not budge when he pushed, nor had he expected it to do so. High above, well out of his reach, was a small square opening and nothing else. The walls either side towered over him, the stones smooth, providing no handholds. His axe was blunt now and in the sack he had only the lemon and wooden soldier.

Oscar lifted the toy free but shook his head. "You can't help me, can you, little man." He started to replace the soldier but stopped. *Wait. That square above can't be an accident. What if... the fountain!* Oscar dunked the wooden man within the water, then lifted it free, setting it on the edge of the fountain. Had it worked? It was a crazy idea but just maybe...

The little man snapped to attention.

"Yes!" Oscar grabbed the soldier and ran back to the castle. "Can you open the gate?"

The soldier saluted, then used his free hand to motion for

Oscar to lift him.

Oscar raised his palm high. The toy performed a quick leg stretch then leapt from Oscar's hand, bayonet outstretched. At the peak of his jump, the soldier drove the blade into the wood, clinging to the rifle, then swung himself up to stand atop it. The fellow's next leap was enough to catch the edge of the square opening, and then he was pulling himself up to disappear inside.

*Hurry, little man.*

A deafening clanking and grinding soon followed. The gates rose, revealing darkness beyond. Light spread into the vast hall, dust motes filtering down from the still-rising gate. Inside, Oscar saw a door half ajar, a pair of giant cog-wheels half-glimpsed within. The little soldier stood before it as if awaiting orders.

Oscar knelt. "Thanks. Stand watch."

The hall was lined with floor-to-ceiling windows and led to a grand staircase, its polished rails reflecting the blue moonlight... Oscar frowned. Moonlight? When had the moon risen? He spun. The light beyond the gate was still the dull dark of evening, but from the windows the bald face of the moon stared down at him. He shivered. *What is this place?*

He raced up the stairs and along the carpeted passage of doors, the faint echo of a muttering voice drifting through the walls. A man's voice. The first door Oscar tried was locked. The second revealed a blue glow, two men standing in place.

Oscar flinched.

Neither man moved. Both were clothed in antique garb, swords belted at the waist, cobwebs spanning helm to hilt.

*Guards?* Their eyes were closed, their faces frozen in the blue light that came from a vial of silver-flecked powder resting in a stand at their feet. Oscar couldn't tell if they were alive or dead, but he closed the door without attempting to enter the light. Several more rooms revealed others frozen and bathed in blue. Some wore servant's livery, others much more regal outfits, and one old man with a flowing beard wore a crown.

Oscar didn't examine the figures long. Instead, he followed the sound of the voice up a flight of stairs to the end of the hall. The faint clap of footsteps preceded him now and the voice seemed to swirl in the stair above.

Silas. The alchemist was climbing to Lady Charlotte with his foul potion.

Oscar ran.

The stair wound on, upwards toward the moon. Finally, he heard a door close ahead and when he reached it, Oscar took a moment to catch his breath before charging inside, ruined axe in hand.

Light poured into the circular chamber from high windows but most of the blue glow came from twin pillars of silvery sand placed either side of a divan, where a beautiful woman lay composed in slumber, the folds of her purple dress covering the furniture. Hair black as midnight, smooth skin pale beneath the moon, there was a kindness to her face that could not be masked by sleep. A furrow to her delicate brow showed distress.

"Lady Charlotte."

"So it is, stranger." The voice spoke from the shadows, dark, rasping.

A man strode from behind the sleeping beauty, his

gaze boring into Oscar with an inner flame. His skin was stretched tight over the bones, cheeks unshaven and lips bloodless. He wore a leather apron and goggles hung from his neck. Small bottles clinked from his belt as he walked. When he lifted a hand to point, Oscar saw the man's gloves were stained with pollen. "I do not know how you passed my forest, nor how you gained entry, but your ingenuity is your folly, sir."

Oscar swallowed, glancing at Charlotte.

The Alchemist frowned. "*She* sent for you? How curious."

"Free her." Anger crept into his voice.

"Ah, so you can speak." Silas wheezed a laugh. "I had wondered. I have watched your people for scores of years and for all your advances you still lack true foresight."

He braced his legs. "Face me now, Alchemist."

Silas raised an eyebrow, then tossed a vial across the room. It shattered at Oscar's feet. Red smoke bloomed. He stumbled back, the momentary exposure searing his eyes and throat. He blinked away tears as a dark shape appeared before him. Oscar lashed out with his axe, connecting with naught but air. Something crashed into his side and he fell to the stones. Silas was upon him, gloved hands at his throat.

Oscar beat upon the man's arms but the alchemist possessed a wiry, unnatural strength. Oscar fumbled for his axe and found nothing, but something bright caught his eye – one of the glass bottles. He snatched it from Silas' belt and swung.

The bottle smashed into the man's face.

Silas roared with pain. Oscar screamed too as the dark liquid within burst free, disintegrating his glove and burning his forearm. He stumbled to his feet. His mechanical hand was impervious to the acidic liquid but it seared the skin of his wrist. When the pain subsided, the crumpled form of Silas lay unmoving, covered in the stillness that only the dead possess.

Beyond the alchemist, Princess Charlotte.

Oscar crossed the tiles with only the sound of his laboured breathing, pausing at the limit of the light. "Lady, I'm here but I don't know how to save you."

Silence.

He sat beside her head, close as he dared. Had the worry lines eased? Oscar examined his mechanical hand. Should he hide it? *No, that doesn't matter now*. He had to wake her somehow. All he had left was the lemon, which had been bruised in the struggle. He lifted it free and looked to Charlotte. "I wish I knew what to do with this."

But maybe he did.

The blue and silver pillars of light and the powder were the things that kept her in her state of sleep, surely? And there was every chance it would do the same to him too, unless...

Oscar fumbled for his tiny belt knife and cut a wedge of lemon free, then extended his mechanical hand into the blue light. At once his eyelids grew heavy but he fought the inclination to sleep and squeezed.

Bitter acid splashed across the alchemist's pillar. The light wavered. *It's working!* Oscar squeezed harder and juice ran through his steel fingers, trailing across the sand. He cut another wedge and sprayed more juice across the powder and then moved to the second pillar where he repeated the process, wringing every last drop from the lemon.

He stepped into the circle of fading light, and his limbs

grew heavy but he bent to lift Charlotte free, laying her across his lap some distance from the divan.

Then he leant down and let his lips brush hers.

Her eyes fluttered and they were such a pale blue that the room faded away to only vague shapes and colours. She took his mechanical hand in her own without flinching and she smiled.

His heart sang.

The White Canyons of Tanakwi

Rone sucked in a breath and inched his Winchester along the grey branch.

Across the canyon, more of a steep gorge, his target perched on a rocky outcrop beneath the hard sun. The figure was unnaturally tall; even as it folded wings around its man-shaped torso, hunched over to gnaw at something. He guessed it over seven feet. The turn of its head obscured a thorny beak and yellowed eyes.

Wind carried a brown feather into the crevice.

He'd always thought them diseased, by the way they moulted and the violent stench of their leavings, but the few times he'd encountered the hawk-men he hadn't been game to find out for certain. *Not planning on asking either, though they'd probably understand more than a few words if I did.*

"Just keep eating, bird-man." Sweat dampened Rone's temples. He itched to shrug off his longcoat, since the dark leather gathered heat so thoroughly it was almost as good as wearing a campfire, but he didn't want to draw any attention. And the shade provided by the wilting grove where he knelt, breathing evenly, might have helped conceal him but it also cut the breeze.

Yet if the hawk-man noticed him… Rone's finger brushed the trigger but he didn't fire. He kept the barrel trained on its body and waited. Finally the thing finished its meal and turned, scanning the gorge before flicking its beak, spots of blood flying, and leaping into the air with a cry.

The shrill echo filled the gorge. Rone lowered his weapon,

tracking it across the pale blue sky, waiting until the hawk-man dwindled to a small dot before leaving cover. He still carried his rifle ready, but the mountains were quiet now; smaller birds and four-legged creatures still hidden away. It would be some time before they re-emerged, certain that the hawk-man was gone.

Rone trekked down a steep trail into the gorge, his boots making their own muted echo. It was cooler at the bottom and he reached out to trail a hand across multicoloured stone walls. Sand, earth and stone were layered, as if some great hand had painted each a different shade; white, a pale orange then a darker crust. A curious effect; people native to the mountains thought the White Canyons were a sacred place, where the Gods came to taste the earth. Apparently the traces their saliva left behind held some magic, something about the 'Path of the World'.

It made no sense to Rone but he didn't argue with them, there was no need.

Doing so wouldn't help him find Tanakwi's young folk either. Sixteen had left and failed to return to the mountain village. Sixteen. Most were children and three were warriors sent after. It was hard to believe; he'd seen them practicing with their spears and bows, joined them on several hunts over the years. And he'd met the young woman who'd been the last to return. Strong, capable, she didn't look like she knew the meaning of the word 'weakness'.

Yet she was bloodied, bruised, desperate to be understood.

"It came from nothing."

Chief Antabo assured Rone that no more than four of their young had ever failed to return from a Maiden Hunt in his lifetime and the man's face carried more wrinkles than the bed sheets of a fever-victim. That the hawk-men were responsible crossed Rone's mind, but they rarely attacked well-armed travellers and the Tanakwi had lived in the mountains for generations. They were hunters. They knew their business.

The final steps of the canyon grew sharp and steep; he had to sling his rifle over one shoulder and climb the rest of the way. At the top more greying patches of grass, his boots stirring dust as he approached a scattered stand of trees. *Just as wilted on this side of the canyon. They're struggling to stay green and they're going to lose the fight too.* He'd seen it all the way up, even in the foothills below.

At the outcrop where the hawk-man had perched Rone found bloodied bones and skin in a pile. It wasn't human. Most likely it'd been a hare, but there wasn't much left. He crouched and rested the gun across his knees. Several hours until darkness fell but he needed every scrap of light; his hunt had been fruitless so far.

Four days he'd searched and nothing – not since losing the trail of the last boy at the mouth of the White Canyons.

His pack still carried enough water for a few more days but Rone would reach the limits of his knowledge about the mountains before too long. Was it wise to press on alone, this deep into the wilds, domain of the hawk-men and other fell beasts? He didn't have an endless supply of ammunition and the only time he'd come so far was when Lyra disappeared.

One hundred and eighty days ago.

Each day since as slow as the last. As empty.

Yet with no traces and no clues it was clear: Rone needed a hunting party. And with just enough water to return now, there was little choice anymore.

He started back down into the gorge.

~~

They were waiting for him on his creaking porch as he walked up the dusty path. The house was just as he'd left it; chimney cold and dark curtains drawn closed, but now the village Soothsayer and Chief Antabo in his long white tunic were speaking before it.

"...I don't know the answer. But I'm tired of checking this place each day. If he doesn't return soon and he's dead, we need that rifle," Hagal was saying, his knobbly elbows waving about as he spoke. His tan tunic rested loosely on his frame; the leather pants too, hung from his body as if made for a larger man. "It's far too valuable. And dangerous, for that matter. What if whatever was killing our young ones gets a hold of it?"

"No man or creature can shoot as well as him," the Chief asked. "Nor will they have access to the ammunition. And how will it solve either crisis? Tanakwi is drying up. Corn is rotting in the fields and the cattle are close behind..." he trailed off when he noticed Rone.

The Soothsayer linked his hands and shielded his eyes against the sun. "Attar has guided you back, Outsider."

"No change here?" Rone asked as he dumped his pack, a puff of dust rising.

"I am afraid not, Rone," Chief Antabo said. He extended a big hand, which Rone took. "The streams are still failing. Perhaps there truly is some manner of blockage where the river leaves the mountain. But like before, no-one has returned from such a search. We feared even you had perished. How did you fare?" he asked, though his expression was not hopeful.

"Poorly. I crossed the White Canyons to the North East, near as far as I ever have but any trail they might have left is gone. I believe we may have to travel deeper into hawk-man territory."

The big man sighed. "Such a perilous journey may have to be set aside, though I wonder if I don't betray the fallen to suggest it."

"The needs of the entire village must outweigh them for now," Hagal said.

Rone folded his arms. "Can you be sure the two aren't related?"

"No," the Soothsayer said. "But that is exactly what we must learn – and you must lead the party."

"Must I?"

"Yes. You owe us, you owe Tanakwi, hunter. We took you in when no-one else would."

"I was only expecting at least a pretence of courtesy in your request, Hagal," he said as he shook his head. "As Soothsayer, I'm sure you've seen that I will do what I can."

Hagal sniffed. "So long as you keep your mind on the task at hand while you search."

Now Rone frowned. "Meaning what?"

"I don't believe I need to explain my words."

"Then let me be clear also; I'd still be looking for her if I thought she was alive and if I find even a shred of evidence to suggest it, I will follow it even to my death." Rone snatched up his pack and brushed past the men, shoving his door open.

Inside, he dumped his pack once more and went to

the basin, resting his rifle across it. Antabo and Hagal exchanged sharp words before footsteps thumped away. The door opened but Rone did not turn. He lifted the rifle and ran his fingers along the barrel, searching for dents.

"He only fears for his village," Antabo said.

"I have not said I will not help."

"That I know; you are a good man."

The door thudded shut. Rone paused to remove his coat, then returned to the rifle.

~~

In the fields, wheat and corn were dying. Brittle traces of their remains stuck to Rone's coat when a warm wind picked up. Beyond the corn, skeletal cattle moaned, many sitting on the dry earth, eyes listless. A dead calf was mired in the silt where a farmer's dam once rested.

He quickened his pace; the village was waiting.

In Tanakwi itself, timber and thatched homes were caked in pale dust. Children playing half-heartedly in the street were covered in dust and flower boxes that held withered stems bore a lining of the same faintly-yellow dust. Washing spread on twine between houses, the bucket teetering on the edge of the well, the windows, the panting dogs and even the ancient clock itself, all suffered an oppressive coating.

The square beneath the clock was overflowing with angry voices. Farmers and frightened villagers shouted at each other while Tanakwi's Fathers shouted down at them from a platform beneath the clock's heavy steel hands.

Rone came to a halt at the back of the crowd. One of the womenfolk, her face pinched and red, was sniggering to a friend.

"They say he's died out there, like his wife. Good riddance I say, high time we were rid of him."

"Too right," the other one replied.

"He was always an ill omen. Remember when Bisa's little uns fell sick and died – that was the day after he came back after his searching."

"Truly."

"I tell you, Samara. I never trusted either of them, showing up from out of no-where all those years ago, *both* with all that blood on their clothes. What do you suppose they were running from, anyway?"

Rone let his shadow fall over them. "Good morning, ladies."

They shrank back. He stared down at them until they moved, then he started pushing his way forward. Whispers followed him through the crowd and up onto the platform, where he faced the Chief, Soothsayer and Filema, the Highway Master. She was a fine woman, an excellent shot, strong, diligent though she'd had little time for him or Lyra over the years.

"Where is my party?" Rone asked. "It should be small, so as to avoid detection. We don't know what's responsible."

Hagal glowered across the space. "I will be leading such a party, Rone. Filema will accompany us as you assist in locating and removing whatever impedes the river. If it is as simple as a landslide, then we will call for help. If it is something more sinister, the village expects you to be ready with your rifle."

A voice called from the crowd. "What about my Ina?"

Similar cries followed, then more shouting as other

people – those who hadn't lost their children – demanded that the river be served first. *Easy for them.* Chief Antabo stepped forward and lifted his arms, calling for order but the villagers and farmers only raised their quarrelling.

Rone unslung his rifle and fired into the sky.

The shot cracked the air. Everyone fell silent, some having thrown themselves to the dirt. *A shame to waste even a single cartridge.* He waited until he was certain everyone was watching before speaking. "I will free the river and then I will learn the fate of your children, as I promised before."

"You? You couldn't even find your own wife!" a man near the front cried.

Rone ignored the sting caused by the words. "Then volunteer to join us."

Silence.

He sneered at the man, then turned on Hagal. "Be ready within the hour; I leave from the northern trail." On his way down, he nodded to Filema who did not acknowledge him, and pushed through the crowd once more.

~~

They hiked through the burnt hills the whole day, walking into the night. The silver moon lit the stony trails, and a thick cloak of sharpica-fur protected Rone from the cool of night. Hagal and Filema were similarly attired. The Soothsayer had wisely kept his mouth closed for much of the journey, since he was out of his element.

Filema too, had said little, her conversation consisting mostly of logistics. In addition to her black-horn longbow and quivers, she carried a barbed spear used for ripping.

Unlike Hagal, she had little trouble keeping up.

Rone stopped before midnight in a half-ring of boulders that offered protection from the wind. While Hagal started their campfire, a luxury they would have to forgo as they neared the hawk-man territories, Rone marked glittering eyes watching from the ridges above. In the clear light of day, the rocks stood in their usual layer of red earth at the bottom, which gradually lightened to brown and then wheat, before ending in a bleached crust. But now they were grey and black, and from within them he heard the sharpicas singing their woes. Long notes of apparent despair.

The creatures hadn't bothered them yet, though he knew they marked their progress. "I will take last watch," he told Filema, who gave a short nod.

Even so, he slept with a hand on the butt of his rifle, the old steel scuffed and worn, comforting beneath his palm.

When Filema woke him for his watch his limbs were stiff but he paced the perimeter of their small camp before settling on one of the boulders, rifle across his knees. In time, a grey dawn grew beyond the canyon ridges and he saw silhouettes; the thin torsos and heavy hind legs of the sharpica slinking away.

They took a walking breakfast, salty jerked meat and water.

"I still don't understand why we don't follow the river more closely," the Soothsayer said after they detoured a patch of thorns. He was already sweating and constantly adjusted his pack.

"This trail is swifter in the long run," Filema said between sips of water from her flask. "It will lead us to easier ground later. Following the river directly from Tanakwi is a tougher climb."

Hagal grumbled but continued on.

At noon Rone came across a siyanna-flower, its slender shape and pale blue petals stark against the stone. The taste of ash filled his mouth as an image of Lyra stole into his mind. She was collecting the flowers, her homespun gown twirling as she danced from patch to patch. He'd smiled then, telling her to save some for other travellers.

Years ago, on the first trip where she had accompanied him into the hills, they'd camped in the peaceful foothills often and never once had he failed to protect her. He gave her a sharpica knuckle for protection against sneak-birds, gave her his pistol to ward off the sharpicas themselves and tried to teach her everything he knew about travelling. But six months ago all his precautions had failed. She went off alone one morning, following the siyanna-flowers down a rust-coloured path by the river, happily collecting her favourite blossom.

Rone had tracked her to the water's edge but found no sign after. All day and all night he searched, before collapsing behind their home, exhausted. When he regained consciousness, he crawled inside, recuperated and started again. For five months he followed the same desperate cycle, until he gave up, empty of tears and even rage, reduced to a gaunt shell whose claws gripped the rifle in an unending promise that he would find her.

One night he'd even wrapped his mouth around the barrel... but hope was insidious; it had not granted him such escape.

Some of it lingered now – the sharpica trail led them finally to the sludge-filled riverbed as it wound down into a canyon. Walls of earth and stone rose around them, stern and sheer. The afternoon sun was soon hidden from sight, plunging the riverbed into shadow. He knelt by the edge, Filema beside him.

"See how it slaughters the fish," she said, poking at a mud-covered set of rainbow scales with an arrow. The trout's eye had yet to be picked over by scavengers – the birds and even the sharpica perhaps wary of the mud.

Only a thin hint of a stream slid through the centre of the river, muddy and slow, aimless. Wind moaned throughout canyon, a deep reverberation.

Hagal glanced to the sky. "The spirits warn us."

"Thinking of turning back, Soothsayer?" Rone asked. The people of Tanakwi thought the high hills near their ancestor's shines cursed, but only since last year when the old Highway Master was found torn in half, his spear missing, arrows unspent and face a mask of terror.

Rone recalled turning away from the river mouth himself on the day of an accidental visit, unnerved by the unnatural silence that had fallen.

But there was no silence now.

"What do the spirits say?" Filema asked, her brow creased. She gripped her spear as her gaze roved the canyon.

"Danger from beneath the earth," Hagal said softly after a moment, then lowered his hands. "That is all. I have lost their voices."

"We have no choice."

Rone rose and started along the path of the river to a cleft in the walls. Where the trail narrowed a stone shifted under his foot. Rone slid into the river with a curse. His legs sunk to the knee in the muck and he twisted for the bank, even as the muck drew him deeper. Hagal and Filema ran forward and the Soothsayer was smiling.

"Take his rifle before it is lost," he told Filema. "We don't need him."

The Highway Master regarded the man a moment before kneeling and reaching down – offering a hand. Rone took it and the woman pulled, muscles in her arms straining, until the river let him go with a squelching sound. He climbed the rest of the way free. "Thank you."

Filema offered a short nod then started along the trail, leaving Hagal to glare after her. Rone stepped close and placed a hand on the man's shoulder, squeezing. "And just how useful do you think you are, Soothsayer?"

Hagal jerked away, starting after the Highway Master.

Rone followed, rifle in hand.

~~

The roar of the falls echoed across the hills.

All afternoon they'd climbed, passing the dome stone shrines, no trace of blood there now, until they stood in the cooling breeze, looking down on a massive basin. It was surrounded on all sides by the jagged heights of the canyons, cast half in shadow. From the hilltops he saw a lone Stag-Tree, black against the dipping sun. He whistled in appreciation of the basin's size. *Was it always this big? It must measure at least two miles across.* A sharp trail had been cut into the side of the walls, winding its way down in ragged, giant steps. *Almost as if the gods themselves built it.*

Crouching by the edge, he examined a set of prints leading down. Large but vague, he was able to make little of them, nor was Filema. "Not sharpica," she said.

He rose to stare down to the basin again. A muddy lake pooled at the bottom of the waterfall. It was vast, but didn't fill the bowl as it once must have. Dark green weeds lay heaped along its banks; pitted holes were visible between silt and stone.

Searching the waterline, he noticed an opening much larger than the others. Partially concealed by the shadows and the waterfall itself, the hole in the wall surprised him. "Do either of you recall seeing that opening, to the right of the fall?"

Filema shook her head and Hagal only grunted.

Did some fell creature lurk inside? Had it been the thing to steal away from its cave, creep up and slash the old Highway Maser to pieces as he rested by the shrine? Had it taken the children – and was it somehow responsible for killing the river? *What if the same thing got Lyra too?*

"If we start now, we can use the last of the light," Rone said as he started the long climb down.

I will find you, Lyra.

~~

The descent took longer than he'd hoped.

At the bottom, dusk had swept in to stain the surrounding peaks red before disappearing, forcing he and the others to crouch at the lakes' edge and wait for their eyes to adjust. Rone stared at the opening, ignoring the muttering from Hagal who had barely stopped to breathe. "And now we're trapped down here in the dark. Exposed! This is madness."

"Climb back, Soothsayer," Filema told him. "Or be silent,

please. I am trying to listen."

Rone smiled beneath the mask of cloth he'd fashioned in order to shield his face from the stench of rotting weed and from something else, a more sinister scent. Different to the hawk-men, somehow more acidic – but foreign still. *Whatever it is, it will taste steel tonight.*

He needed the moon to rise so he could examine the opening and get out, with or without the others. A sense of urgency had been building and it was hard to shake. *I'm close to an answer, somehow. I feel it.* While he sat, the hunter flexed his muscles to keep his circulation up. He was loath to move around too much, lest he draw unwanted attention. Somewhere out there the sharpica were prowling, waiting for easy prey, and somewhere beneath the rock, just as Hagal's spirits claimed, something waited.

Finally the moon climbed high enough to turn the water to restless silver. *A fleeting moment of beauty.* "I am going inside," he told Filema, whose bow rested across her knees. "If anything follows me, kill it."

She caught his arm as he made to rise. "Are you certain?"

"Let him go if he wants to," Hagal said.

"Yes," he told Filema. "Thank you." He did not look at the Soothsayer as he started forward, levelling his rifle at the gigantic opening. He kept to the driest parts of the bank, avoiding treacherous mud and heavier clumps of weed. The roar of the water thudded against his chest, clogging up his ears. Rone strained his eyes. In the black, he thought he caught a glimpse of moonlight on something wet. His finger touched the trigger in a reflex movement, but he didn't fire.

It was only a flash; after all, he wasn't even sure he saw it, now that it was gone. Rone was barely a dozen yards from the opening now, his eyes fixed on the darkness. He stumbled and risked a glance over his shoulder. Almost unconsciously, he'd detoured a pit, but hadn't noticed the ground sloping on its other side.

Examining the earth, he found that the depression was unnatural; its sides were torn and crumbling. *Almost like a print.* Another rested nearby, this one much closer to the water's edge, and much deeper. It was about the same size, and ended in tips that the first did not.

Rone reasoned that his body would fit inside the print. He shuddered at the thought of the creature's size, gritted his teeth, and moved up an uneven slope. Even from his slight vantage point he was able to see the prints for what they were.

Webbed feet.

Gigantic webbed feet, leading from the lake's edge directly to the cave.

Rone strapped the gun onto his shoulder and started back toward the others. One rifle was not enough.

~~

"It is only a theory," Rone said as he finished. "You can see – there is no blockage at the fall itself. Water still reaches the basin, but goes no further. The level has dropped dangerously, as though something or someone is draining it slowly from beneath."

The Soothsayer frowned. "But that doesn't answer who or what could possibly do such a thing? Or why they would even want to do so?"

Rone shrugged. "As to the who... don't forget the

monstrous prints. Their owner would dwarf the clock in Tanakwi."

"And something cut Olda in half," Filema said. "It makes sense to me. A predator is defending its territory. Maybe when Olda was sent to investigate the befouling of the shrine, he came too close to discovering the creature's lair."

Rone nodded. *And maybe the creature is why Lyra disappeared too.* Still he had no proof for such a thought, had nothing but a feeling that would not fade.

Before Hagal could reply, Filema shouted a warning.

Rone spun.

A pair of sharpica bore down on them. *Damn them!* The hill-beasts were spitting and hissing as they charged. Hackles up, club-like forelegs outstretched as their powerful hind legs propelled them into the air, one crashed into the Highway Master.

A wet crunch filled the air. Filema fell the ground, her skull split by a blow from the thick, bone-covered foreleg. She hadn't even had time to lift her bow.

Rone dove from the second beast as it landed before him, hissing, yellowed teeth pale in the moonlight. He tore his hunting knife free, slashing at it, keeping the thing at bay. His rifle lay beyond the creature, near the Soothsayer. The whites of the man's eyes were clear.

"Shoot them," Rone shouted. "What are you waiting for?"

The man dashed forward, lifted the gun and pulled the trigger. The shot rang out, followed instantly by a sharpica's squeal. The beast facing Rone turned to flee at the sound, its feet thumping along the hard earth. He watched the animal gather itself for a mighty vault, then leap into the distance, landing hard and driving itself into the night air once more as it fled.

Rone sheathed his knife and moved to Filema's body. Blood ran from her ears, one side of her head dented. *She didn't deserve this.*

The hunter took her bow and handed it to the trembling Soothsayer after relieving the man of his Winchester.

"I hope you can shoot, Hagal," he said as he lifted the first stone of what would be Filema's cairn.

~~

Rone split his attention between the sun-lit lake and the enormous opening where he rested behind a mound of weed that he'd built into makeshift cover. He'd included a slime-encrusted branch that he'd wedged into the clumps, setting the barrel onto the rough Y shape of the branch.

Hagal stood beside him, sweating heavily and stinking of body odour, though how Rone could smell it over the putrid reeds was a miracle. *Doubt I smell any better.* He thanked the Mists that they were downwind of the giant opening. Mid-morning had come and gone, and noon was fast approaching – it seemed his plan was going to fail.

For long hours they'd stared at the sharpica corpse. Both men had taken turns dragging it across the uneven ground to its current position where it rested over hot coals before the entrance as bait.

Hagal waved his hand at the cooking meat. "It's not working. We've had it there for hours."

Rone sighed. "The wind *has* been uneven. Either that or the creature isn't hungry, or it's too smart."

"So what do we do?"

"Well, I'm not spending another night this close to its lair."

"You mean for us to go inside? Are you so eager to die?"

Rone scratched at the growth of a beard. There was a chance he'd find a trace of Lyra, he was sure of it. *Either that or I'm fooling myself.* He'd packed lamps along with their food, water, blankets, fire-making tools and weapons. "The village deserves answers."

"We are no match for it."

"We can't just sit here all day. There's little cover, and we can't draw it out. Besides, once it's dark we lose the element of surprise."

"You think we can surprise it? We don't even know what *it* is!"

"If it sleeps during the day, we just might surprise it."

The man was silent for a long time. "When we lure it out what do we do?" he said at last.

"Once we have it out in the open, you draw its attention away from me. Shoot it, curse it, sing to it, whatever, just so long as you give me time to get off a good eye-shot," Rone said as he tied his mask and started across the space between their hiding place and the opening.

At the jagged entrance, the creature's strange, wet odour was strong despite their face coverings. Taking off his pack, he removed the lamp and lit it before entering the lair, the Soothsayer close behind.

"It is only you and I now, Hagal," he said, glancing at the man. The fellow nodded and from his look of fear, Rone supposed the Soothsayer probably wouldn't try another stunt like the one in the mud.

The tunnel interior dwarfed Rone, though its roof sloped

steadily, following the passage downwards. As he walked he strained his ears for unnatural sounds. The pale glow from the entrance was soon a useless spot, the only illumination coming from his shuttered lantern.

When Rone signalled a halt, the dripping of water was loud.

"What's wrong?" Hagal asked, breathing muffled through his cloth mask.

"We're close to something." Rone strode on until they came to an antechamber.

A floor-to-ceiling iron door dominated the room. Rone sucked in a breath. The strength needed to move such a slab... It was both amazing and terrifying. *Who did this? The creature? Humans?* Pale blue light snuck from a crack where the door hadn't closed. He approached it slowly, dimming his lantern and motioning for Hagal to follow. Peering through the gap, he let his sight adjust.

"What do you see?" the Soothsayer asked.

"Wait for me here," Rone whispered, handing the light over and squeezing through the door. Hagal did not follow and Rone found himself in a seemingly limitless cavern, standing on a giant's balcony complete with a giant's handrail.

The blue light came from a lake that covered the cavern's floor. He stared, holding his breath. It pulsated and moved with a hypnotic quiver, most unlike water. Thousands of tiny but intense balls of blue light floated up from the lake's surface, disappearing into the black roof.

It was vast, so much vaster than the hills of Tanakwi. "More like the entire land." Unwittingly, he'd spoken aloud. It was like a pulsing ocean beneath the world, its horizon the distant black of the underground. A liquid humming reached his ears. He paused; it came from below. Peering over the rail, he saw a crudely cut opening. From it trickled water. *So the basin above is emptied to feed this new lake? This is killing the river? What creature would need its own drain?*

A slimy arm shot from the centre of the lake and he flinched.

The arm absorbed a number of the floating balls and when it smacked back down to the surface, a violent wave spread in expanding circles. Further on, he saw another arm do the same, fingers grasping. To his left, another, and he finally understood.

The blue phosphorescence was alive.

He took a slow step backwards. Had the blue mass sensed him? A hundred – a thousand – eyes seemed to have turned his way. Rone continued to back toward the door and a chill ran through him.

*This thing couldn't have made the prints outside.*

~~

Rone crept along the balcony, his rifle cocked.

Keeping to whatever shadows he could find, he came across yet another door, this one just as large as the first, but wide open. He paused. The drip of water was audible, like a thunderclap when each drop hit stone, that and the faint humming.

He stepped within and was confronted by a row of glowing stone wells set in the ground. Stout but wide, he estimated their openings to be close to twenty times bigger than the village well.

"By the Mist, what is this place?" he breathed.

The first well looked to be filled with blue glass. He extended a trembling hand and let it hover above the surface; no heat, no chill. He lowered his palm. Beneath a thin sheen of sticky liquid, the surface was rock-hard. Inside the next one, Rone frowned at a human-like shape, appearing as a child in a great tomb. He shuddered; the man was completely still. *Was he frozen alive? Is this one of the youths from Tanakwi?*

Rone drew his belt knife and scratched at the substance, failing to make even a tiny scratch. Trying to shatter the surface was too great a risk, even if he did think the pommel of his blade or the butt of his rifle would be strong enough. *Sorry, friend.*

Sapphire shards crunched beneath his feet as he leant over the next well. The sides were caked with pale slime. There looked to be no bottom.

Of fifteen wells, only one contained a man and only one was broken. The rest were full of glowing blue liquid, which he dared not touch. *Does the monstrosity below take men for servants? Or food?* He shook his head. *No. Something mobile made the prints outside and the same thing diverted the river, surely.* "And the wells..." The wells were involved in the creation of beasts. And the beasts helped the grand liquid mass steal water, on top of keeping nosy villagers like Highway Master Olda away.

Possibly the youths too.

Rone returned to the occupied well, a dark hope stirring. *Could Lyra be in one of these things, trapped somewhere in this enormous cavern? Am I a fool even to consider it?*

The sound of slapping footfalls scattered his thoughts.

Rone spun from the room and sprinted along the balcony where he threw himself through the door. Hagal jumped, Filema's bow clattering to the stony floor. He snatched it up. "What's that light? And the noise?"

Rone grabbed the lantern and shoved the Soothsayer up the tunnel. "It's coming!"

Distorted shadows splashed across the walls as he ran, lamp swinging wildly. Rone stumbled several times, but the grinding of the iron door spurred him on. The creature would be in the tunnel with them soon but he dared not look back.

"It will have to run crouched over, we can escape," Rone called.

"How do you know?" Hagal gasped out.

"I just do!"

Rone cast the lantern aside when the tunnel entrance appeared. Sunlight pressed into his eyes and he squinted against it, pushing his body harder. When he burst free he scrambled up the rock face to his vantage point above the entrance. Hagal tried to follow but Rone shoved the man back down. "Distract it. Trust my aim."

The Soothsayer dashed across the uneven ground, keeping some distance between he and the opening where he raised Filema's bow and set an arrow to its string.

Rone caught his breath, letting the thumping of his heart slow too. *You need a steady arm.* He heard the creature; faint beneath the waterfall at first. Its webbed feet sounded as though they were cracking the very stone. *I'm not prepared for this.*

But the creature hurtled from its lair in a blue flash. It locked its gaze onto the first thing it saw – Hagal.

How had it even managed to exit? The thing was so tall and so wide. Part fish, part frog, part blubbering blue mass, its face was a contortion of razor-fangs, gills and odd human features. Most disconcerting were the eyes; they looked totally human.

And he recognised those eyes, could never forget them, no matter how enlarged or watery they had become.

The monster was Lyra.

A bowstring twanged. An arrow hit stone. Hagal was backing away, panting. Luck had granted him a killing shot against the sharpica but the Soothsayer was no archer. He fired again, this arrow thudding into flesh. But the creature did not pause. Rone lowered his rifle arm as Hagal backed away. Sharp fins on the end of long arms lashed out and he avoided them only by falling.

He was screaming for Rone to shoot.

A second later the sweep of a fin cut the man in half, leaving his entrails scattered across the rocks.

Rone lay his rifle down and waited for his wife.

~~

Only her eyes were the same.

The rest of her body was a mass of blue flesh, a distortion. An abomination too, something that should never have come to be.

And yet it was Lyra.

*I know it, I know her eyes.* The day she'd gone missing; she'd stumbled into the underground cavern and fallen prey to the thirsting blob somehow. Or maybe a different creature had taken her from the river? It did not matter. Rone wept tears of bitter joy as his Winchester clattered to the stone. "I searched for you." He reached out to touch one of her fins, remembering how soft her hands had been, but the cuts they made now stung like salt.

She gave no answer, only stared down at him with her enormous green eyes. He tried to explain, to apologise for giving up, tried to beg her forgiveness but it was all for naught, his voice faded to a hoarse whisper and she did not answer.

Only her eyes spoke and there was a joy within.

Rone started toward the opening, taking the weary, relieved steps of a traveller long away from home.

Into the dark of the tunnel Rone went, taking no light, and passed through the open door, guided by the cavern's glow. In the chamber of wells, he saw Lyra through his tears, the way she looked when they first met, in the honey-field, in a land far, far from Tanakwi. She had been working to protect the saplings, making little walls from stakes and hessian cloth.

Her smile of satisfaction had made him smile.

He wore the same smile as he climbed into the broken well. Blue gunk invaded his ears, his nose and his mouth and his chest quickly grew tight but he welcomed the pain, welcomed the blue silence.

All the while, she watched him

Never *(Prequel to The Amber Isle)*

Air rushed from Never's lungs as the brute landed another blow.

Never choked on a curse as he doubled over. The two other guards lifted him again, grip tightening further. "I can't help feeling... there are other ways to tell me... Lord Firmita is busy," Never gasped as he glanced up to the leader's silhouette. The man was a hulking figure before the torchlight that caught in the warm breeze and twisted across stony manor walls.

There was not much to see, just two glittering eyes in a darkened face. The man's lip would be bleeding too, courtesy of Never's elbow.

"Search the fool. Knife him if he gives you any trouble."

Rough hands snatched the pack from Never's shoulders. Another man searched his vest and the inner pockets of his cloak, removing several knives and tossing them to the grass.

Damn swine.

The rebuke could have been directed at himself – he'd misjudged them. Quite clearly his story of meeting Firmita in the garden had been pretty thin, especially now that he was being robbed by the man's guard. Given a chance, Never might still talk his way into a meeting with the lord of the manor and find what he needed.

Unless his blood got free.

Then, no amount of talk would make a difference. But so long as they didn't cut him, everything would be fine. Offer no resistance, let them search. Keep calm.

The empty purse at his belt elicited a curse from the leader. "You've got nothing." The big man spat. "No gold, no silver, nothing."

"I'm just as disappointed as you," Never said.

The man folded his arms, muscles bulging beneath the edges of his tunic. Red and yellow strips appeared near black in the night but the white from the rest of the tunic seemed bright enough to shave by. So clean. How did they manage it? Testament to Lord Firmita's fastidiousness, perhaps.

One of the fellows holding Never sighed. "Let's just take him to Firmita already. He's obviously worse off than us."

"Good idea," Never said. "After all, we wouldn't want him catching his men robbing a guest, would we? He's rather devout, as I understand it."

One snorted. "Guest?"

"Wait a minute," the guard holding his pack said. "What's this? Diego, want to take a look?" Never sighed when the man carefully lifted a wrapped relic then unwound the cloth to reveal a hunk of carved stone shaped as a fish.

Or so it seemed at first glance.

The fellow frowned down at it. "It looks old."

"Good guess," Never muttered, unable to stop himself.

"Shut your mouth," the leader, Diego, said as he waved the men closer.

In the yellow glow of the torchlight, carvings on the piece of stone glittered – the granite he'd worked into the surface to mimic scales and more, to mimic the old relics once commonly found near the Sand Cliffs. The way the guards' eyes lit up suggested it had fooled them – but would it fool their lord?

And would Never even get a chance to attempt his

ploy? After trying for weeks to arrange a meeting with the collector, some boldness had seemed in order... but there was boldness and there was foolishness.

"Now this we can sell," one guard said.

Diego shook his head. "No chance, Bu."

"Why not?" Bu whined.

"Think you or I know the first thing about what it's really worth? Or who to sell it to?"

Grumbling.

"Put it back." The leader flexed his hands, balling them into fists as he began to pace in and out of the torchlight, clean-shaven jaw working. Finally, "Search him for more knives then take him to see Firmita."

"What if he talks, Diego?" the other one asked. "You know, about us robbing him."

"If he tries that, leave it to me. If I say he's an assassin, Firmita will put him in the cells. Once he's there I'll kill him and blame it on the other prisoner."

"Charming," Never said. And just why had guards taken up thievery?

Diego flashed an evil grin before stalking off into the darkness.

One of the guards kicked Never in the back of the knees. He fell, cheek thumping against the grass. Never growled. No matter how neat Lord Firmita kept his grounds, there was nothing to be done about the immediate itch.

Bu held Never's own dagger against his throat while the second fellow searched, finding the knife strapped to the small of his back.

"We can sell a few of these at least," Bu said.

"Not being paid well enough?" Never asked.

"Diego said shut up," the other guard snapped.

"Just one more thing – you forgot my boot," Never said.

The man grunted as he shuffled down to remove that blade too. That was all of them and it might build some trust, which he needed if he was going to survive long enough to get a proper look at Firmita's collection of ancient relics.

Would his luck hold?

On the other hand, he was inside now, and sometimes that was half the battle. Being captured and unarmed made everything more difficult, admittedly, but life tended to be dull without challenges.

And he *needed* to see the lord's collection. The legend of the Sunken City might just be real after all, and one of Firmita's maps marked the location. Or so rumour held.

"Up with you then," Bu said.

Never stood, allowing his hands to be bound with coarse rope that dug into his skin, and then stumbled forward when the men pushed him toward the light. Beyond the first torch waited a heavy door leading into the manor, which Bu thumped upon. Windows above offered no movement, no light.

Silence followed.

Bu beat against the wood again and waited. Still no response.

"Perhaps they're sleeping something off," Never said.

"Keep quiet," the other guard muttered.

When the door finally opened, a man waved them in without apology or explanation, ignoring a curse directed at him by his fellows.

A dim corridor of stone stretched to a distant staircase, twin lamps casting a pale glow across two figurines. When his escort reached the stair Never raised an eyebrow. Twin rearing stallions flanked the steps. Both brass and both polished to such a high sheen that he had to fight a childish urge to smear one with a handprint as he passed. Firmita was beyond fastidious – he was perhaps obsessed; why else ensure such attention to detail in what had to be a minor entrance to the manor? The man was hardly going to admit the Empress via such a passage.

At the top of the stair Never was shoved along a narrow passage of wooden-panelled walls, again dimly lit, and finally into a small room with table, two chairs and a cold lamp, which Bu lit.

Then the two closed the door and the sound of a key rattling in a lock followed.

"No parting words, then?" Never asked.

Silence.

He paced. Firmita would doubtless arrive in moments, which meant Never would soon find himself within reach of another clue, thrown outside, or sent to the cells with the other prisoner. Which was odd. Why did the Marlosi lord have a prisoner? Any serious crime would have been dealt with by the Imperial Guard. Was something afoot? If so, it sounded like the sort of business Never ought to avoid.

But choices were few and far between these days.

After years of dead-ends and rumours, he finally had something to go on.

The manor held another clue: outside of the Imperial Palace, Firmita's collection of relics from ages past was among the finest. Priceless. Of course, the gold didn't matter. But the sunken city of Quisoa, if real, might hold another piece of the puzzle on the twisted road to discovering the truth behind Never's curse.

Perhaps even his true name.

"One thing at a time," he muttered.

Footsteps approached. Never lifted his head expectantly as once again a key turned in the lock. The door swung open and two men entered – Diego, his face now set in an expression of neutrality, and the Lord of the Manor.

Not a single silvery hair appeared out of place on the man's head and his beard too, the colour of iron, had been trimmed to a fine edge. His sunken eyes were even ringed by just a touch of kohl – typically a woman's embellishment, or, as was growing fashionable among the nobility it seemed, something only for the very rich. And very vain.

He carried the fake relic, which he set upon the table before motioning for Never to sit.

Never did so. "Thank you for seeing me."

"This is a fair forgery of an ancient rockfish relic," Firmita said without preamble, his voice hard.

"Ah." Trouble.

The man frowned. "You do not deny it. What was your purpose with this?"

Never sighed, drawing it out. The truth would not win him any favours. "Gold. I am fallen upon hard times and this was my final ploy."

"I see." The man stood. "I hope Pacela will grant you mercy. Nevertheless, you will be imprisoned until such time as I have to call the Imperial Guard."

"That is fair."

"What is your name?"

"Never, My Lord."

The man stiffened. "You refuse me?"

Never raised his hands, still bound. "Not at all, Lord Firmita. But that is my name: Never."

Firmita studied him a moment before motioning to Diego and spinning on his heel. The guard hauled Never back into the hall, where Bu and the other one waited with frowns. Escape was still a problem – but not the first. The first was time. Firmita appeared curious now, and that was a bad thing. Curiosity meant watchfulness and if the Lord rushed through whatever it was that kept him from sending for the guard or resuming questioning...

Forced back along the dim passage and down a flight of stone steps concealed behind a hidden door, Never was led to another darkened room. Bu had brought the lamp and its glow revealed a row of cells – half a dozen perhaps. Few appeared used, as dust and webs covered many. A shape lay huddled in the corner of the nearest cell.

Diego opened the adjacent cell, pushed Never inside, clanged the door shut then leant against the bars as he untied Never's hands. "You did the right thing back there so let's keep it that way, Never, or I'll be back. Understand?" he said. "You keep your mouth shut."

Never offered no answer.

"Did you hear what I said?"

Still Never said nothing.

"Answer me, scum."

Nothing.

Diego's nostrils flared and he reached for the cell door. Never grinned. "I thought you wanted me to keep my mouth shut."

The man shook his head and spat on the floor before storming out, taking his fellows and the light with him.

Never chuckled as he waited for his eyes to adjust to the darkness. Even breathing from the other cell suggested his fellow prisoner was not waking any time soon, since he – or she – hadn't so much as stirred.

There was little light to adjust to. Clouds seemed to have covered the moon and barely any starlight slipped through the dusty strip of a window high above. He could just make out the grass but other than that, there was nothing to see outside and little reason to climb up and look. Without losing a lot of body mass, he wasn't squeezing through. Nor would anyone with a chest broader than a hands-width.

Never gripped one of the bars – steel cold against his palms – and gave it a shake. Nothing. He moved on to the next one; same result. But when he reached the last bar his fingers found the grit of rust. "Ah." Never twisted the bar, a grinding sound his reward. He continued to work, jerking it, then twisting further and stopping for periodic kicks.

It was working.

The bar was coming loose. He stepped back and aimed a good kick at it. A shock travelled up his leg but he kicked again, then returned to twisting and wrenching the iron. He soon worked up a sweat, removing his cloak and continuing until the bar gave a powdery snap at the base.

"Perfect." Almost too easy – that was the beauty of old cells. There was always a weak point.

He retrieved his cloak and squeezed between the wall and remaining bar before creeping toward the faint suggestion of the door. He ran his hands along the wood but the handle would not budge. If he waited for someone to feed him he could escape but until then he was still trapped. Could he try wake his fellow prisoner? Break them out, ask for help?

Light bloomed beneath the door.

He fell back but the door was already being unbolted. It swung open and lamplight blinded him even as he shielded his eyes.

A woman's voice spoke, a hint of surprise within. "There you are. Quickly, come with me."

~~

"I am Julesa, Lord Firmita's daughter."

He blinked as she lowered the light. The fine features of her face were creased with impatience, her dark eyes seeming to absorb the light. Her black hair had been pulled into a bun and a single silver clip adorned her head. She waved a bejewelled hand from her long-sleeved white robes. "We must hurry."

"I agree but I have to ask why you're here to... rescue me?"

"That window is shrinking with every wasted moment. Follow me." She strode from the room.

Not unlike her father, was Julesa. Never leapt after her, catching up to the light and matching her stride. "What's your plan?" he asked.

"For you to be silent while I get you out of here."

"Wonderful. How assuring."

Julesa did not answer. Instead, she paused before a wall and depressed a hidden switch – possibly with her foot, since he did not see her hands move. A panel slid open and she stepped in then glared at him. "I told you, we need to hurry."

"I might like to take a look around first," he said. There was still a chance he might find a map or some other hint before escaping. After all, he'd already gone through the trouble that came with being captured and divested of his knives, the least he could do was discover whatever secrets lay within the manor.

"Are you a fool? Father will have you hanged if he realises you've escaped."

"Everyone dies from something."

She hooked the lamp on the wall and lifted something free, levelling it at him.

Crossbow.

Never winced as he raised his hands. Vadiya make, and in good order too, if the way the limbs gleamed was any indication of its condition. She held it like she knew how to shoot.

"Would you like to choke on a bolt?"

"Only if you don't have anything softer."

"Enough playing the fool. If you made that forgery, you must have some brains at least. Use them now."

He folded his arms. "Then convince me or shoot me, dear lady."

"I'm breaking you out to send you to the city. I need you to stop something happening. If you agree, I'll take you beyond the wall. If not, I'll simply shoot you now."

Never grunted. Killing seemed to be everyone's favourite answer to any problem around the Firmita manor. "What do I stop?"

"An attempted robbery – Father is transferring some of his rarer pieces to loan to the Imperial Gallery."

"A thief to catch a thief?"

"Indeed."

"And you know all this how?"

Her eyes flashed. "That does not matter – you will take

my word or die."

"Difficult choice. Can you guess what I'm thinking?"

"Of course – what's to stop you simply agreeing now, escaping and washing your hands of the matter? You could easily disappear."

"You know your scoundrels," he said.

She laughed; a cold sound. "I do." From her belt she lifted a pouch and hefted it. The clink of coin followed. "Isn't this what you live for?"

"I do enjoy gold."

"Then if we have an arrangement, follow me."

He trailed the glow of her lamp into the passage and down a stair before entering a cellar. Crates of figs and pears were stacked along the walls, casting looming shadows. Julesa paused by a pair of barrels and gestured to them with the lamp. "Make yourself useful."

"Lucky for you I'm so good-natured," he said as he strode forward to wrestle first one, then the other barrel aside. Beneath waited a trapdoor, which he lifted. Steel rungs descended into darkness. He stepped aside. "Lead on."

Lady Julesa started the descent and Never kept within range, a chill rising from below.

He stepped into a rough-hewn passage where damp seeped through the walls. Did the passage run beside the manor's well? Julesa walked on without comment until they reached another ladder.

"We're beyond the walls now. The tunnel opens into a small stand of trees," Julesa said. She climbed swiftly now and at the top, doused the lamp before opening a hatch to the warm night air. Never climbed out after and crouched within the trees.

The manor's yellow glow rose over nearby walls, but no guard walked the parapet and no sound of alarm leapt out into the night. Julesa was already counting out coins, which she tucked into an inner pocket in her robe. The purse, now well over half-empty at a guess, she tossed to his feet. "You get the rest when you stop the theft."

"That occurs when?"

"Three nights hence," she said. "They will attack a covered wagon at midnight, before it enters the palace from the artisan's gate – do you know it?"

"I do. How many?"

"A team of five – I trust that in addition to the gold I have given you, you have resources of your own you might call upon?"

"Enough."

"Good. I will be watching," she said, then removed two knives and threw them too, to the dirt, before starting back down the ladder.

"How much are they worth?" Never asked. He had to – she'd expect it; and more, he couldn't fight a touch of curiosity.

"A great deal." Her voice echoed.

He closed the trap door with a snort and scooped up the knives – one of which was his own, the bone inlay a giveaway – and the purse. Only a single piece of gold within when he tilted it to the moon where its light fell between the leaves. Not a king's ransom but better than a crossbow bolt to the face.

Never started toward the road where it cut a pale line through the gently stirring grasses, east toward the capital. At first, he passed no-one on the road, which suited him well. The hush and the steady thud of his boots on the dirt was company enough.

His plan had failed but new opportunities were afoot in the... uncharitable motives of others, often one of the best places to look when it came to finding opportunity. For Julesa's offer did seem rather fraught with risk.

No doubt she herself was behind the plan to rob her father.

During the robbery, the 'true thief' would be killed but the relics would not be recovered, nor would Julesa herself. It would be hinted that the thief had done away with her somehow and all eyes would turn on the corpse and not the shadows where she – and whoever was helping her – were quietly slipping away.

And who better to be the 'true thief' than Never – a man who'd recently attempted to dupe the Lord himself, and who had escaped.

It was a clever plan – just not clever enough.

Tomorrow, once he reached Isacina, there would be time to decide just how to deal with Julesa. If at all. He frowned up at the moon. Of course, there was still a chance those relics *could* tell him something, especially if the map he sought was there.

And didn't it have to be? Quisoan relics, especially pre-Empire pieces, were indeed among the rarest.

Never chuckled. "Opportunity indeed."

He walked until the moon disappeared and only a whisper of starlight remained above, at which point he left the road and sought a depression, resting there with his cloak for a pillow.

A few hours' sleep would be enough. His limbs grew

heavy now that he'd stopped, and when he closed his eyes, echoes of Julesa's face swam before him, sometimes smiling, smug and haughty, sometimes weeping, her eyes wide.

~~

The sun beat upon his face when he woke, throat dry and sweat already forming.

He stood with a grunt, shaking out his cloak, sending grass seeds flying across the plain. Before him, the golden crops of Marlosa's central lands spread in a shimmering haze, Folhan Mountains a dark shadow looming beyond. At its feet, hidden yet, lay Isacina – the white city and the seat of Empress Crisina's power.

Isacina, where all manner of folk from the Empire and lands beyond brought their wares or sought their fortunes... or, sought other people's fortunes. Despite the diligence of the Imperial Guard, there was a sophisticated criminal world within the city. A world Never had brushed up against enough times to wonder whether Julesa had help from the Brotherhood.

A wagon crunched along the road, dust clinging to its sides. A farmer taking his wares to the city? Never jogged after. If the Brotherhood was involved, he'd keep them out of the way somehow. Right now, a ride would be welcome.

And water.

"Greetings!" Never called, waving to the driver.

The farmer lifted his straw hat and raised an eyebrow but didn't slow his old grey. "Morning."

Never kept pace. "Are you heading to the city by chance?"

"Near enough. Collecting another load of pears from the

Walija farm."

"Wonderful – would you be willing to take me so far?"

"Might do." He wiped his brow. "So long as you don't mind keeping quiet – I'm not much one for talk."

"Understood." Never climbed up beside the man and leant back against the wooden seat. The crops rolled by with only the wagon's wheels crunching on the road and the occasional snort from the horse.

Eventually, the farmer took a drink from a flask. He offered it to Never, who drank. Sweet, still-cool water. "Thank you."

Around noon, a trio of crows burst from the fields when a horse galloped down an intersecting road, this curving around toward the imperial city. When they reached the crossroads, the farmer pulled his horse to a halt. "Here's your stop."

Never hopped down. "Thanks again."

The wagon drove on and Never turned after the horse. The walls of the city were within sight now; pale monsters looming above. More horses and caravans passed him, dust covering their hems or wheels and many of the people with songs on their lips – mostly those young ones in small groups, dressed in their best clothes as they trekked to see the capital and its wonders. Caravan guards with their mismatched armour and unshaven faces did not smile as much, but there was always another job.

At a crest, Never paused, leaving the road to remove his cloak and stow it in his pack. It didn't make a huge difference, but it was enough to ease sweat as the sun grew more oppressive. The flow of people, their voices filling the blue sky, passed on, sliding down toward the huge stone gates that had been flung open to welcome all visitors.

Those that first built the city – three brothers, hired by an old king if he remembered correctly – knew how it would dominate the view from the crest, as it likely did from the other roads flowing into Isacina.

White and grey stone set in layers, climbed to the sky. First the forty-foot wall, and then beyond it, the circular towers of the palace and the great winged spire of Pacela's temple, taller even than the palace and its glittering domes. Glass flashed in the tiny windows that climbed the spire and dotted the white wings. A beautiful view, if one was lucky enough to climb it.

Finally, the ancient Twin Oaks of Ashina – the green tips of their leaves standing like spears over the walls just beyond the gate. Planted by the Goddess of Spring herself, or so the legend claimed. Maybe it was true; he hadn't seen oaks of such majesty anywhere else.

Never re-joined the flow of traffic, passing a pair of young men discussing the wonders of the Pink Rose. They obviously had no idea what the girls of the Rose were willing to do, but the staff would soon set them straight if the lads even worked up the nerve to approach the gilded gate.

A merchant in a fine coat lectured an apprentice or son on the value of grain and its role in Marlosa's economy, and the thunder of hooves announced a squad of Imperial Guard, their breastplates bright in the sun. The riders' white cloaks snapped as they passed, the emblazoned red stallions appearing to rear up. The crowd parted for them as they returned to the city. Some folk knelt in deference and others grumbled as they were forced to tread through the ditches.

Progress slowed. Ahead, the crowd squeezed through the

gates and Never frowned as he waited. Nearby, a bald man shook his head. "Can't they build a second entry already?"

Never offered no response. A shout of frustration – a young voice – rose from before the walls. Laughter swelled in the crowd. The cry of annoyance changed to a yelp of pain. Never frowned as he skirted the edge of the crowd.

Two boys – not quite men – were shoving at a shorter lad dressed in a motley of yellow, red and green, with tassels on his sleeves and huge ivory buttons on his coat. His eyes blazed with fury and a raised red mark already marred his cheek. He was reaching for a rag doll held by one of the older boys, raised high, out of reach.

Whenever the younger neared, one bully would toss the doll to the other then cuff the short lad across the head when he turned to follow the doll.

The crowd still laughed and jeered, but a few muttered darkly to themselves.

The lad was beginning to grow desperate, fists shaking.

Never strode forward and kicked one of the young thugs to the dirt. "Greetings," Never said.

The bully shot to his knees, his expression one of outrage. He spat dirt as he lifted a quivering finger, his narrow features twisted. "What do you think you're doing, old man?"

The motley boy and the one holding the doll had frozen, mouths agape.

Never grinned. "I'm not that old, son. Now, how about you give up your game and go get drunk until you vomit a river in a nice, cool alley somewhere? Or would you rather I gave you a real thrashing – that includes your bovine-faced friend, too."

The lad pushed from knees to feet. "What'd you call him?"

"It's a peculiar word, isn't it? It means he looks like a cow, which I think is better than you; cows are placid and I have to admit, you look a little like a rat to me." Never kept his voice pleasant.

"You're going to regret saying that." Rat charged, Cow a moment behind.

Never leapt to meet them.

The move caught both off guard. Never ducked under a wild swing from Rat and drove his fist into the lad's ribs. The young man collapsed with a whoosh of air as Never then twisted away from Cow's knife thrust.

Never snapped his hand over Cow's wrist and spun the boy around, jerking his arm up behind his back until it popped from its socket. Cow screamed. Never dumped him to the dirt, kicking the knife away. Rat was still groaning.

Never glanced to those nearest in the crowd, who had fallen largely silent, many with faces turned away. Perhaps for the best, and he was lucky. If blood had been shed and his curse broken loose, he didn't fancy being chased down to the chanting of the words 'freak' or 'monster'.

"Obviously I won't be able to do this sort of thing for everyone," Never said. "So please, don't get any ideas now." He turned to the boy in the strange clothing, who was retrieving his doll. "Are you well?"

A nod.

Shouts for order broke through the crowd and half a dozen Imperial Guard shouldered their way from the gates. Swiftly, they encircled Never and the young men, spears and swords in hand. The leader, a captain by the sharp, hooved insignia on his cloak, folded his arms.

"Surrender your weapons at once – you are each to be

imprisoned for brawling."

Never sighed.

The price of helping others.

~~

Never stared up into the branches of one of Ashina's giant oaks, the lawn soft beneath his feet as he waited for transfer to the nearest prison. People detoured around both he and the colourfully-dressed boy – tied together, and ringed by steel. The bullies and their own guard were stationed nearby but had little to say.

No surprise there.

Red-breasted robins flitted amongst the branches, their chirping adding to the hushed sounds of awe from visitors gathered around the mighty trunk, its bark gnarled with age. A peace had washed over him, the way it always did when he stood beneath the tree; and it had been a long time – not since he and Zia spoke here last.

"Thank you, sir, for what you did back there."

The boy looked up at him.

Never offered a brief smile. "Well, I can't say it's worked out very well for either of us but at least you've got your puppet back." Now that he was close enough, the ragdoll bore more the look of something crafted. It was a hand-puppet and its face was carven bone, a grinning imp, skin tinted blue.

"It was my father's," he said, round face darkening. "I cannot afford to lose it; it is my livelihood."

"You're a jester?" Jesters were rare – not something the Empress seemed to care for, but the old kings were said to have used them.

The lad shook his head. "No. And nor will I be, it seems. My father was jester to King Yecapla but now that he has died and the Imperial Minister has taken over, there is no call for someone like me."

"Sorry to hear it, lad," Never said. Yecapla's dominion was one of several smaller kingdoms once covering Marlosa and the surrounding islands. After being unified, many kings held their titles but became no more than governors bowing to the line of the Empress – Ramakki differed in that when the line of its king died, an Imperial Minister took control.

"My name is Temilo," he said. "I thought maybe I could find work as a performer in an inn here but I hadn't even entered the city when those two started."

New guards marched up to their group and Never found himself passed into their hands, and then the new men were dragging them up a street, Temilo stumbling after. Two and three storey buildings – mostly inns or shops, their white stone striped in yellow or red – blocked both the sun and palace, but Never caught glimpses of Pacela's Spire as they crossed the cobblestones of an intersection.

Wisely, the guard took them along quieter streets and eventually into one of the smaller jails. Cool within, the building was little more than a squat box with barred windows. There were perhaps a dozen cells in all, most occupied by drunks and youth with the ragged look of pickpockets.

Two jailors sat at a desk spread with playing stones, the small piles roughly even. They stood when Never was pushed forward.

"Hold them until morning," one of the Guardsmen said.

"Will do." The first jailor herded Never and Temilo into one of the empty cells while the second continued to speak with the guard. Never rubbed his neck as the cell clanged shut – how unpleasant that such a sound was familiar.

Never sat on one of the cots, leaning his head back against the stone.

His stomach rumbled.

Temilo, who'd been examining his puppet for damage, glanced over at him from his own cot. Never grinned. He rose and approached the bars. "I don't suppose you feed us, do you?" he called to the men, who'd resumed their game.

"No," one snapped without turning his head.

Laughter from the other cells.

Never returned to his cot. Nothing to do except wait for morning. He lay across the bed and stared up at the ceiling; a piece of stone had been repaired in the distant past, the mortar set in the rough shape of a hammer.

Temilo leant forward on his cot. "Sir, might I ask your name?"

"It's Never."

"Never? Forgive me for saying, but that's a strange name."

"I agree."

"And are you a travelling warrior?"

Never gave a soft chuckle. "I'm travelling, but I usually try to stay away from fighting."

"I'm not sure I understand, but I'm glad you were travelling today."

Never sat up again. "Tell me about your puppet. I don't recognise the design. It doesn't appear Ramakki."

Temilo smiled as he held up the hand puppet. "See the eyebrows, how thin they are? Father said that it is from the old line of Ramakki Kings but the peaked hair comes from the islands north. The blue skin is for the Ramakki God of Truth."

"And does he bear a name?"

"*Sorga*. It means 'truth-speaker' in the Ramakki language."

"A risk-laden business, the truth."

"It is," Temilo said softly. He placed the puppet within one of his pouches and took out a piece of string, which he wove into a pattern around his fingers. Temilo fell silent as he worked on the patterns and Never lay back again; no need to bother the lad.

He dozed until evening, when he woke to a dark cell. Temilo was asleep and when he moved to the bars, new guards sat beneath the lamp. Never called softly. Tomorrow would soon be upon him and it wouldn't hurt to learn a few things to prepare – one of which was decent accommodation – and now that the empire had generously donated a bed, four walls and a roof, he might be able to afford one of the nicer inns long enough to interrupt Julesa's heist.

One of the jailors groaned then hauled himself out of his seat.

"What is it?" he asked when he came to a halt outside the cell. His eyes held a look of weariness, but he seemed more fit than some of the jailors Never had encountered.

"What does a room at the Water Petal cost a man nowadays?" Never asked.

"Think you could afford it?" The jailor said with a raised eyebrow.

Never palmed a gold coin, then spun it across his knuckles. "Once I'm out of this delightful place I intend to find out. You might be able to save me some time."

A grunt. "That'll only last you two nights."

"And that's all I need, thank you," Never said, repressing a sigh. Prices had jumped somewhat since he'd last stayed there.

"You don't look like the usual sort we get in here," the guard said, his curiosity apparently stirred. "You don't even stink of wine."

"Not much of a compliment but I'll take it," Never said with a grin.

"So, what's your story?"

"I'm trying to set up my nephew with work and I thought the Petal might be looking for entertainment."

"The Ramakki boy?" the guard's expression was sceptical.

"He's a jester. And he's older than he seems."

"Then do right by him when we let you out of here," the man said before turning back for his game.

Never sought his bed once more and lay back, closing his eyes to the darkness. Getting a decent rest wouldn't hurt... yet he couldn't help shifting on the cot. Some uncertainty lay ahead. Would Vento still work at the Petal? It had been years now. The man would remember him – saving someone's life made that rather a given – but that didn't mean the innkeeper would necessarily be willing to share the information Never would need.

After all, his livelihood depended on the thieves patronising his business; he couldn't simply give up whatever information Never asked. Still, meetings might be arranged.

But not until tomorrow – and a long tomorrow it would likely be.

~~

Never paused before The Water Petal, standing in the shade of a fruit vendor as a pair of white-cloaked Imperial Guard half-pushed, half-carried a limping beggar out of sight. The woman's face had been a little smudged with dirt but her clothes were cleaner than many – and she'd had a pleasant enough voice that she hadn't used to badger passers-by.

The city's blasted vanity was growing worse if they were moving beggars along.

He'd left Temilo before the jail, directing the lad toward the old guild of performers with wishes for luck, and while the boy's face had not grown much more confident, he did walk with more of a spring in his step.

"If you aren't planning on buying something, go away, will you?" a voice demanded. A small man with a pinched face waved a hand at Never from behind the counter of the fruit stall. "You're bothering my customers."

This early, few people were about.

"Very sorry," Never said, and spun to walk away, knocking peaches to the ground as he did. Cries of outrage followed but he ascended the steps before the inn without looking back. The Water Petal offered a broad roof of canvas, sheltering its open doors from the sun. A painted sign revealed a lily pad floating in a pond, and the words 'Welcome Wayfarer' were written boldly.

Instructions for sweeping and other chores – someone wanted the windows cleaned too – echoed from inside. Was it Vento's voice?

Within, Never bypassed rows of tables and chairs with their floating candles in central bowls, each dark now, to approach the long bar where two figures spoke. One was a young woman in an apron. "She never does any real work around here, you need to –" She lowered the cloth she'd been waving when she noticed Never.

"We're not yet open, my good fellow," the barman said, then paused to squint. "Never? I can hardly believe it." There was more white in the man's dark hair than when Never last saw him, but it was Vento – his crooked nose and rough voice unchanged.

"I missed your nose," Never said as he took the man's hand. "Who is your lovely assistant?" he asked.

"Serni," the woman replied with a raised eyebrow. "And part-owner is more like it. Are you here for work then?"

"For help, actually," he grinned.

Vento laughed. "That's no surprise. Serni, would you wake Lina and have her bring us something to break the morning's fast?"

"Only if you agree to talk to her – give her a piece of your mind for a change."

Vento sighed but nodded before waving Never around the bar where they took a door into a corridor lined with more doors. Vento passed them all, turning to an alcove where a heavy, oaken door with an ornate lock waited.

"This looks new," Never said.

"It is – I wanted more room." He produced a key and admitted them, gesturing for Never to take a table beside an open window. It looked out to a walled garden, shadows cast by tall trees.

The scent of fresh-cut flowers lay heavy across the room, which was dominated by a large painting of Pacela. Never studied it while Vento rummaged around, removing a stack of books from a chair. In the painting, a beautiful woman rose from a field of grain, her golden robe matching that of the field, blonde hair flowing as if in a breeze. The Goddess, watching over the land.

"Here, take this," Vento said as he placed the chair at the table and sat across from it. Never joined him as the man continued. "You look like you've travelled around the world twice."

Never shrugged. "Maybe just the once. I spent a lot of time in Vadiya, dancing with Steelhawks."

"Your search?"

"Right."

"And that's what you're here about? You think I can help you?"

"I do. You hear things, Vento – you'd know if anyone was planning to steal something really valuable. Like ancient relics visiting from Lord Firmita's estate? I think I'd like to get a look before that happens."

Vento grinned. "I haven't heard anything like that. But if you want to speak to someone who might, I can see if they'll meet. It'd take a few hours."

"How about I go for a stroll around the markets?"

"Then I'll arrange it. And if you want a room, you should know I've raised my prices."

Never sighed. "I've heard."

Vento barked a laugh, slapping Never on the shoulder as he stood. "Come, let's go see about breakfast."

~~

After a hot meal of spiced eggs, Never walked one of the markets while waiting for noon – when he would meet with Vento's contact in the thieves' guild. The sun beat down, baking the dust of old stones. The small amount of shade offered by a vendor's canvas was usually filled with people, and being pressed between sweating, arguing folk wasn't his idea of respite.

Still, he purchased replacement knives with some of the money left over from Vento's fee and glanced over other wares too. Little tempted him and he found himself gradually growing aware of the weight of eyes upon his back.

Someone watched him.

Pausing beside a weaver's stall, he knelt as if checking on his boots and glanced around the market. People in white robes with slashes of yellow and red or sometimes blue... mostly Marlosi folk, but enough pale-skinned Hanik from the eastern forests to stand out too. Yet no-one appeared to be paying him any special attention.

Old foes perhaps. His last visit to Isacina had left a few people rather unhappy, but enough to be watching for him now? Merely a day since his return? It was a big city – the Water Petal was barely beyond Ashina's trees, and he'd not come close to the Singing Quarter where there had been a misunderstanding with the bard, nor the warehouses where Never had nearly lost complete control of his blood during a nasty knife fight.

But by noon he'd learnt nothing and headed back to the Petal to wait for Vento's man.

The common room was crowded but a table had been saved. He took an empty seat and ordered ale. While he waited, he toyed with one of his new knives, testing the weight and balance. Without them, he often felt naked, exposed. Was it odd that instruments of death offered him such comfort? Why not? His blood was cursed, after all.

Conversations drifted to his table; boasting, arguing, murmurs of the Empress finally choosing a consort. Nearby, a pair of men spoke softly, excitement tightening their voices.

"No. It's not how to get to the Amber Isle, I know that. It's where to go once you're *inside*," one man said.

Never tilted his head slightly. The Amber Isle? A treasure-hunter's myth according to most – but if it truly existed it too might hold ancient secrets. Gods knew he'd tried to chase down all the others. Many had searched and few returned from the Isle but all agreed it was an old legend even before the first War of Dust, two hundred years past.

The other man scoffed. "Think you're going to find the Sea King's jewels, do you?"

"No, *we* are," the man said. "I've been to the Grey Chain, there's a way to the Isle. As I said, all we have to do is find the map."

"If it exists."

"It does – I heard it from Neosi. He used to work in the palace library before he tried to double-cross the Brotherhood."

"Neosi you say?" The second man paused. "Now that changes things. He was sure about what he saw?"

"Of course."

"Any ideas about how we'll break in?"

The first man lowered his voice, glancing over his shoulder. Never continued to toy with his blade, as if unconcerned by his surroundings. The fellow grunted. "Not here. Meet me at the palace tonight, I'll show you."

The two stood and left. Never exhaled softly.

Another clue or a fool's path?

Serni appeared, holding his ale. She placed it on the table and sat across from him with a smile. "Well?"

He raised an eyebrow. "I admit you are more pleasant-looking company than I was expecting."

"You're only half right, Never. I'll pass on your request – the guild remembers you and your... unfortunate affliction."

Of course; they'd remember his curse well. Never grinned. "It's not catching."

"Nonetheless, let's hear what you're looking for and what you're offering."

"Fair enough." He outlined Julesa's 'fear' about her father's relics and paused to drink. "So you can understand I'd like to know if the Cofradia has any stake in the heist – as that would change how I approach the situation."

"And your offer?"

"A generous cut of the reward for its return perhaps. Say, two thirds."

Senri gave him an appraising look. "Two thirds? What are you playing at?"

"Information."

"Ah. You think these relics can tell you something about your curse."

"Believe me, the money is not important. Take four fifths, I care little."

She folded her arms. "All this is dependent upon there actually being a reward for their return. That is nothing you can guarantee, so we will have to decline."

"It's 'we' now, is it?" he asked.

She didn't address his question. "Offer something else."

Never drummed his fingers on the tabletop. Quite the request. What could he offer? All he possessed was his years, cursed blood, his clothes and a few knives. "I have so little, as you might imagine."

"What of your skills?"

"Such as?"

"Death," Serni said. She leant forward. "The ones assisting Lady Julesa seek to establish a base here in Isacina, and the Brotherhood would be happy to help if you were willing to disrupt those plans."

"Surely they don't need my help with such a thing?"

"Of course, we could drive them out but the Marlosi and Quisoan relics change everything – we hardly wish for royal attention. And more, why do the dirty work if someone else will do it for you?"

"I see. You have an arrangement with Firmita and cannot publically be seen to break it. Hence my services."

"Aren't you clever."

Never leant back in his chair and waved a hand. "Very well. Tell me about Julesa's friends. How many, how organised? Where and when will the attempted theft happen? I might be clever but I'm not fond of surprises."

~~

Never crouched in the depths of shadow on a rooftop, his breathing even as he listened. A wagon rattled on the street below, nearing the artisan's gate. The gate's carved panels showed men and women at work building Pacela's Spire. Midnight cast a silvery-blue tint across the carvings and the square but it was the buildings opposite he studied.

The attack would come from within. Five men, as Julesa claimed, would rush the wagon before the gate opened – which it wouldn't, seeing as the guards had been paid to keep it closed.

All this Never knew, but still he fought the rush of adrenaline.

His own plan relied on some delicate timing of its own.

He glanced beyond the gates. Hints of the palace itself, overlooking the city from its hill, were shadowy in the night. Its towers dominated the skyline even though few lights glowed from its rows of windows. The scale of it always offered a little thrill – so many rooms. No doubt it took an army of servants to run.

The unpainted wagon finally rolled into the square. Two men only sat at the driver's seat, a covered crate behind them. "Luck be with you, men," Never whispered. He slipped along the roof and swiftly descended his rope, then ducked into the recess of a doorway. Movement across the square caught his eye. A glint of moonlight on steel.

The driver leapt down with a grunt, sword swinging at his belt as he approached the heavy gate and rapped upon the door with the knocker. The sound echoed across the night but no-one answered. He knocked again.

Feet thundered across the square as men charged from the shadows.

Never swore – ten men, not five!

Had he been betrayed?

Not now.

Odds had to be evened. And quickly. The curse... there was a chance he could manage it without calling his blood, wasn't there? The wagon guards were already reacting, moving to protect the relics as two more men burst from cover in the back of the wagon, but even with the two men he'd hired, it still left five to take down ten.

Never charged, knives in hand.

Shouts rose over the clash of steel echoing in the square. Never ran to the first man that had engaged his hidden troops and slashed his knife across the thief's back, spinning to dodge a blow from another of Julesa's men.

The man sneered as he swung again, and Never danced further back. He feinted and rolled into a crouch, slashing the man's knee as he passed. The fellow collapsed with a shout. The coppery scent of blood filled the night. Never growled when his own blood stirred within his veins.

No.

On his feet again, he flung a blade at a man who'd raised an axe over his head. It pierced the thief's side, just beneath the arm. Never didn't see him fall – he was already running for another struggle, a new knife in hand.

A loud snap rang out.

Pain tore into his forearm. Blood sprayed as he stumbled several steps. He clamped a hand over the wound as he ducked into a crouch. Something whirred as it passed overhead.

Julesa stood across the square, reloading her crossbow.

Clever bitch.

Never switched course, throwing a dagger as he did. Julesa deflected the blade with her crossbow. But he closed the space before she could reload. He knocked the weapon from her grip with his good hand. She went for her own knife but he backhanded her to the stones, chest heaving.

Julesa's eyes blazed and blood ran from her mouth.

Fool!

His own blood shot forward in a black stream. Attracted to the crimson, his curse surged, eager. It struck Julesa and drew forth her own lifeblood. She screamed, desperation clear in the wild note. Never jerked his arm back, breaking the stream, but it was too late.

Her own blood continued to pour free as she struggled to stand, reaching her knees before collapsing. Blood pooled around her head as her scream became a cough, then a gurgling sound as she choked.

Never's stomach twisted as he slammed a hand over his arm.

Too late, too late.

She was dead – nothing could stop the blood. And worse, something of Julesa passed into his own, into him – as it often did with the curse. Her panic wracked his limbs, but more. Memories came unbidden. Julesa and a young man with a shock of blond hair. They laughed and spoke of running away together, of escaping her father and his oppression. An older man next, Marlosi nobility, and her hatred of him was clear – a marriage she did not want.

And so she and her blond lover hatched a plan to steal her father's artefacts. He knew someone in the city and she knew Firmita's route –

A cry of despair cut the connection.

Steel clattered to the stones.

Never spun.

The blond-haired man from her memories collapsed beside her, cradling her head. Julesa was still now and her expression offered some hope of peace in death. Or so he wanted to believe. Never met the blond man's eyes and there was only horror within – somehow worse than judgement.

The sound of fighting had ceased.

The young man choked out a sob and lifted her to walk from the square without a single faltering step.

Death, that was all his curse was good for. How he loathed it! Why had the Gods punished him so? Why? An answer he would not learn, it seemed. Perhaps not ever. Never turned back to the wagon with a heavy tread. Bodies lay around the wagon – most of them appeared to be Julesa's men. One of the wagon guards lay slumped against a wheel, groaning as he tied off a tourniquet above his thigh. Never tore a strip from his cloak and did the same, covering his wounded arm and pulling the strip tight with his teeth as best he could.

The other driver, Diego, stood with the mercenaries Never had hired. That left six bodies on the stones, meaning at least one man had fled. Perhaps at the sight of Never's curse. The three standing men approached Never.

Diego spoke first. "I have to thank you, Never. Didn't believe you about the attack at first, but I'm glad you found us in that bar; we'd be dead otherwise."

"Happy to see you alive."

One of the mercenaries grunted, the one with the heavy beard. "Look, that's all well and good but we need to be paid. And as soon as possible – Imperial Guard will be here soon and I have no intention of sticking around." He narrowed his eyes. "Nor staying near you, friend, if you understand."

"I do," Never said. A common response from those who witnessed the curse in action – at least this man had the courage to follow up on his payment. The other mercenary still had wide eyes and looked away when Never glanced at him. "Let's open the crates then."

Diego took an iron bar and popped the lid of the nearest crate open. He unpacked the first piece; a Marlosi carving from ancient tombs at a guess, and then another, handing it to the bearded mercenary with both hands.

"This is a hunk of stone," the bearded man said, voice flat.

"No, it's a rare and valuable headpiece from the tombs in the Didecolla Mountains," Never replied. "Imperial property, technically. Worth twice its weight in gold. There are at least five people here in Isacina alone who'd take that off your hands, no questions asked. My only advice is that you and Diego sell to different people – you know who to try first," he told Diego, who nodded.

The other mercenary stepped closer. "Let me see." He held it up to the moonlight. "It looks real to me, Guena."

Guena grunted. "And you'd know?"

"My pa used to take me to the museum when I was young. I recognise the old runes." The second mercenary handed it back to his leader. "We can confirm it later. I don't want to hang around."

Gunea pointed at Never. "This better be real, else I'm coming to find you, blood or no."

"It's real."

The mercenaries strode off into the darkened streets, weighed down by their earnings.

Never moved to the second crate while Diego divided up the remaining pieces between himself and the other driver, Juqe. Never took a deep breath. Within could rest another clue, more answers, hope. Please. He set the cold bar against the lid and wedged it in. Nails squeaked on wood as he pried the top free.

He set the bar down and lifted out the first piece.

Another Marlosi relic, a statue of Pacela when she was still believed to possess two faces. The next two pieces were minor religious deities; he placed them with Pacela. "Quickly," he told himself.

Finally, closer to the bottom, a steel case – was it the piece he was looking for? It had been protected well enough, slid between other pieces and shielded by a wooden frame. Never smashed the lock with the butt of a knife and opened the lid. Carved into a shard of stone, an old map of Quisoa – pre-empire.

Here he would find the true location of the sunken city, and within, knowledge of his ancestors, surely? No links to his Marlosi heritage had borne fruit but Mother had been Quisaon; there *had* to be something there to explain his curse.

Surely in the sunken city of Quisoa, if no-where else?

Never tilted the stone to the moonlight.

And everything was the same, the same as any other map of the southern empire.

The sunken city did not exist.

It likely existed only in the wild, empty rumours of folklore. Another dead-end. Another trail of clues gone to dust, scattered now. Never gripped the stone until his fingers ached.

Just a shred of hope, by Gods, please.

His shoulders shook but he did not hurl it to the flagstones. Instead, he replaced it and closed his eyes, exhaling slowly.

Somehow, he had to find the strength to start again. Which meant finding another legend and following it as far as he could... like the dozens of times before. And yet, this time, hadn't defeat left at least a little opportunity in its wake? He spun in the wagon, waving to Diego.

"I need your help."

The man exchanged a glance with his fellow. "Look, we owe you but like the mercenary said – we aren't sticking around."

"I only want you to seal me in this crate then explain to the Imperial Guard what happened – you shouldn't have much trouble selling your story – just make sure they get this wagon inside. Then you can disappear, like you have to rush back to report this to Firmita."

"What?" Juqe frowned. "Why would you want to do that?"

"So I can sneak into the palace."

"You don't want your share of the relics?" Diego asked.

"Take mine, just get me inside," Never said.

"Consider it done," Diego grinned. "Help me hide this stuff first."

Never carried some of the pieces into the shadows and once finished, climbed into the near-empty crate. Diego replaced the lid, thumping the corners into place. "Won't be long – I hear a few sets of boots."

"Good." Never adjusted his limbs as best he could and waited in the pine-scented darkness.

When the troop of guard paused in the square – spreading out and demanding answers, Never tensed. Would they really buy Diego's story? It wasn't a difficult tale to spin...

"You two put down this many alone?" a guardsman asked.

"We already sent two others off to get a healer," Diego said. "Look, we just want to get back to Firmita and tell him what happened. Maybe it was personal, maybe not. Can you guarantee my Lord's wares from here?"

"Could be Brotherhood, Captain," a guardsman called from across the square.

The captain grunted. "Fine. On your way, we'll get the wagon inside."

"Maybe I should stay and be sure," Diego said, his voice affecting concern and just enough distrust to make him sound angry and petty. Never had to give him credit.

"We can manage," the captain said.

Shouts rose for the gate to open, followed by thumping. Then swearing, until the captain sent a runner. Never shifted, awfully slowly, while he waited. The plan had worked – but it was taking them entirely too long.

Footsteps rushed closer. "Captain Remaso, something's happening – I can smell smoke."

A new voice. "There. It's coming from the eastern wing, it's a bloody fire!"

The captain swore. "We have to get this inside now. Bande, go wake the city watch and clear the wells."

More crashing on the gate, as if someone had taken up a piece of stone.

Finally it screeched open and a voice shouted. "By the Burning Graves Below, what is going on?"

"Where have you been?" a voice snapped back.

"Taking my watch, friend. I only heard your hollering by accident, so clam it up, will you?"

"Where's the gate guards?"

"A fine question."

Captain Remaso intervened. "Figure it out later – there's a fire. I want this wagon within, it's a shipment from Lord Firmita. Everyone is to deal with that fire, understood?"

"Yes, Captain," the voices chimed.

The horse snorted and finally the wagon rolled forward.

Never flexed his hands – some luck at last, yet he still had to get into the library and find the map to the Amber Isle somehow. Before the thieves from the Water Petal, and before the threat of fire, too.

Although, the chaos would provide good cover – it always did.

~~

Never crept along dark corridors, pausing before every intersection, door, or stairwell as he neared the Great Library. Escaping the crate had been easy enough, even without light. The Imperial Guard had rushed off the moment the gates boomed shut behind them, leaving Never to slip through silent marble-floored halls.

Now he slowed at new shouts.

Calls had been drifting across from the opposite end of the palace grounds but they were ordered shouts for action and watchfulness. From a window, he'd seen the red glow from what he estimated were the stables.

But these new cries were filled with shock.

Steel on steel followed.

Never frowned – some of the voices called for more swords, some for reinforcements, for commanding officers, some shouts urged people back into their rooms.

And he hissed when he realised some of the shouting was in the Vadiyem tongue.

What treachery was afoot?

The stairs leading down to the vaults of the library were unattended – instead, two Imperial Guards lay in their own blood. One man's eyes were rolled back into his head but the other wheezed, his gauntleted hands wrapped around a crossbow bolt.

Never flipped knives into his grip and dashed forward. "Who did this?" he asked.

"They came from nowhere," the guard managed.

Never hesitated. Either the Vadiya had attacked the palace, attacked Marlosa – or a few Vadiya were after something in the palace or the library. The fire seemed to suggest a diversion – but whatever it was, it was no half-hearted attempt.

He had to leave.

At best, he'd be mistaken for being involved; imprisoned after the attack was dealt with. At worst, he'd be killed by the Vadiya or Imperial Guard in the fighting. Yet he did not budge. Chaos. The best time to sneak in and out unseen. There was a chance he'd stumble across something to make up for his failures – perhaps even a map to guide him within the Amber Isle.

Footsteps thundered up the corridors leading to the library.

Vadiya soldiers – not just regular infantry but Steelhawks, laden with bows, daggers, hand-axes and swords – poured into the hall, their armour catching the torchlight. The leader pointed at Never and one of his fellows reached for a bow.

Never spun down the stair, bursting through the broken doors of the library and skidded into the shelves. They stretched beyond the limits of the lamplight, each like a glowing pool in a world of musty parchment and leather bindings. Only his breathing rasped as he ran deeper. The chance of escape was not in his favour – he couldn't take on that many Steelhawks, even with the curse. It was useless against them. For the most part their armour protected them from the kind of cuts Never might inflict to use his curse.

Instead, he'd have to hide and wait. Take a chance. Slip behind them once they spread out. The Great Library was nearly an entire city block in width and length, a dozen men would not find one, if that one were quiet enough.

And Never considered himself quiet indeed.

He controlled his breathing and slowed his steps, crossing into a new row and backtracking enough so as not to lose the exit, where he leant against a giant shelf and strained his ears.

No need; the Vadiya Commander snarled his orders and the Steelhawks split into pairs. Each group took a lamp and ensured one man carried a drawn bow. Never rolled his shoulders; so, they weren't going to make things easy. Typical.

But just what were they doing in the palace? In Marlosa? It was a question he couldn't afford to answer, but it nagged him as he slipped between another set of shelves and drifted closer to the exit. It was still several rows distant but he was drawing parallel with the first pair of Steelhawks.

Movement flashed between the shelves.

Two figures ran for the stairs. Steelhawks shouted and arrows snapped – both running figures crashed to the ground. Library attendants or palace folk seeking a hiding place?

"Well, who are they?" the leader snapped as he walked over.

"Not guard, Commander Harstas. They look like thieves."

Never slowed; the two from the Water Petal?

The commander sighed. "Very well. They are dead, yes?"

"Soon will be."

"Then spread out, find the other one."

Never kept still. The Steelhawks resumed their search. Not until the light faded did he move again, approaching the thieves. Neither stirred, one facedown and the other twisted on his side, scroll case gripped in hand.

He knelt beside the man's outstretched arm and opened his fingers, lifting the case. He twisted the top and let the scroll within slide free. Glancing to the receding figures often, he looked to the map.

A maze of passages was revealed. Skulls marked some corridors; a spoked wheel, another. The scroll was old, frayed at the edges, and its ink fading but he could see enough. Was it truly a path to treasure? It *felt* right but he couldn't say why. Something about the scent of age, the flow of the words...

He'd searched every other ancient ruin it seemed, spoken with healers and folk who claimed to know dark magics and it all yielded so little – yet something had placed him in the path of this map. Maybe not the Gods, maybe not fate but he was no fool when it came to following coincidences.

Tucking the scroll into his belt, Never stood.

A shape hurtled toward him.

Vadiya.

Never caught a knife-wielding arm as he hit the stone floor, the man's weight knocking the breath out of him. But he kept a grip on his attacker's wrist, reaching for his own blade with a free hand, even as he gasped for air.

The man shouted for help and Never growled.

He drove his head forward, smashing into his attacker's

face. Pain bloomed but he hurled the man aside and found his feet. He skipped away from a grasping hand and then kicked the man before the soldier could get to his knees. The Vadiya clattered back to the stone.

An arrow ricocheted from the wall near his head and Never flinched back.

Men surged forward, drawing near from many sides.

Slow them down!

Never leapt for the nearest shelf and hurled his weight against it.

Wood creaked and the huge shelves began to tilt. Two of the Vadiya closed in and the commander, his red cloak inky black in the dim light, skidded to a halt as Never gave the shelf a solid kick.

Books slid free and the shelf crashed down – but not before the commander used one of his men as leverage, hurling himself back to safety while leaving his subordinate in the path of danger.

The Steelhawk disappeared with a muted cry, crushed beneath huge shelves.

When the wood crashed into the next shelf it knocked that down too, scattering more soldiers. Never cast one of his knives through the clouds of dust and another body clattered to the ground – he'd taken down the fellow with no helm.

Not a bad throw, considering the poor light and dust.

Then he was charging up the stairs.

Once at the top, he ran down the corridor, heading for the nearest stairway. Distance. He needed to lose them first. Then find the quickest path out.

"This way," someone cried in Vadiya.

Never skidded around a corner; glanced back. Two Steelhawks, closing the distance despite their armour. Bastards trained from birth, why wouldn't they keep up? He reached for a statue – a heavy brass figurine of a rearing stallion. Then he waited at the edge of the corner.

Feet thundered closer.

Just before the first Steelhawk came into view, he swung the stallion.

A mighty crash filled the corridor, shockwaves travelling up his arms. The second man tripped over his friend. Never dumped the statue and drew a knife, plunging it between the gap in the man's breastplate and helm.

Blood spurted but Never was already spinning away, batting aside a lunge from the first man, who still lay on the floor, trapped by the weight of the corpse. Never stomped on a grasping wrist and drove his boot into the man's head.

A crack and the Vadiya was still.

Never paused to exhale; his luck held.

Something hot sliced into his thigh. He blinked at the sudden flow of blood. Another two Steelhawks charged along the corridor, one drawing a second arrow. Never fell back, scrambling to pick up speed. Along another corridor and then up a stairwell, grunting with pain as he slid into a small armoury, complete with a window overlooking the grounds.

Never snatched a halberd from a stand and rammed the butt through the window. Glass shattered. Voices echoed up the stair. Never strode to the top and drew the halberd back and waited. Blood trickled down his leg and his chest heaved.

A Steelhawk appeared.

Never drove the weapon down with a roar. The point pierced the man's breastplate and cast him back, knocking his fellow down the stair with a hideous crash. Never ran for the window, ignoring the scrapes he earned when he slipped through, gripping the edge of the sill and kicking around for a foothold.

Something firm rested beneath his boot.

In the dark it was impossible to tell what, but it seemed to take his weight. He stepped down and clung to the minor imperfections of the stonework. The edge of a turret was near enough that he could reach across and brace himself between the sharp angles. The strain on his arms and legs was immediate but he worked his way down, passing an ornamental bust of Pacela.

Moving as swiftly as he could, Never soon reached a balcony. Leaping down, he paused to tear another strip from his cloak and bind his leg as best he could. Two wounds now, and blood was seeping through the bandage on his arm as well. He glanced up. A head peered out from the window.

"Down, down," a voice cried.

Never swore, then kicked in the door to whatever room lay beyond.

West side of the palace – not guest rooms, generally these were reserved for minor nobles. Someone gave a shout from an adjoining chamber, but Never took advantage of the moonlight streaming through the now open balcony, finding his way to the door. He opened it and paused. When no arrows came he peered out.

Empty corridors. The sound of battle from the left. Imperial Guards were fighting with Vadiya – Harstas' men or other Steelhawks? Never took the opposite direction, soon coming to a darkened stairwell ahead.

Worth a shot, especially if it got him safely to ground level...

Harstas appeared at the opposite end of the passage. He shouted a Vadiya curse and charged, several of his men in tow.

Never dashed for the stairwell.

~~

Inside the stairwell Never half-ran, half-stumbled down. One hand trailed the wall as a guide. At the bottom waited a storeroom, door open and lamplight glowing. Never leapt inside and a robed man jumped, his eyes wide as he looked up from a ledger.

"Who are you?" he stammered as he fell against a crate.

"You must flee," Never said. "Quickly, is there any way from this room?"

The man dropped his quill. "What is this about?"

Never caught the fellow by the shoulders. "Listen to me now. If you want to live to write another number, tell me. Can we leave this room – not the stairs."

The man trembled. "Well, yes. I mean, there's an old access to the aqueducts in with the cold goods but no-one –"

"Show me."

The man tripped over his own feet as he turned to lead Never into the next room but Never caught him. "Quickly, there are men chasing me."

The stock-keeper ran for a door and led Never through row after row of fruit crates packed between barrels of water. Near to the rear of the room there rested an iron handle on a hefty-looking hatch in the floor. Never pointed. "That?"

The man edged away. "Yes. It leads into the aqueducts. For cleaning."

"And it travels beyond the city?"

"Yes."

Never bent and took a firm grip on the handle. "Don't be rusted shut," he told it before heaving. Nothing. He pulled until his arms shook and it started to grind open. He kept the pressure on, using his legs, his whole body to lift, letting it clang open against the stone. Then he stood back and caught his breath, wincing at the way his wounds throbbed – only to be interrupted by the slapping of feet on stone. "No, not that way," Never cried after the scribe.

The man hollered something.

Never took a few steps after. The fool had already reached the stairs. He started up then screamed... only to come tumbling back down. The cracking of bone echoed in the room and Never flinched.

Harstas followed, flanked by two men. The commander had lost his helm and his pale skin and blond hair were tinted yellow by the lamp. With little more than a sigh of annoyance, Harstas ran the scribe through and wiped his blade on the man's robe before rising, meeting Never's gaze.

Never unlocked his clenched jaw. One of his knives was already in hand – he charged and threw, piercing the visor of one Steelhawk. Low on knives, he ripped a small box from a stack and hurled it at the other Steelhawk.

It exploded, spraying peaches everywhere but the man faltered only.

Harstas waved his subordinate forward with a sneer.

Never gave ground to the longer reach, deflecting

blows with his remaining knife. He was in trouble. With little room to move, he had to do something. Beyond the soldier before him, Harstas was lifting a bow from his fallen comrade, fitting an arrow to the string.

"You're finished," the Steelhawk said.

"Good to know," Never replied, leaping back. He took advantage of the extra space to whip a cut across the back of his hand. Then he bounced on the balls of his feet, letting the Steelhawk approach.

Before the man could get within range, Never dove forward, sliding between the fellow's legs. He slapped the stone to halt himself, slashing at the point where his enemy's greaves were buckled.

Leather snapped and blood flowed – this time Never let it spray forth.

Yet the man still twisted to swing a downward blow. Never rolled. The point of the sword caught his shoulder – and more blood shot forth. The Steelhawk fell back with a gasp of horror. He crashed into the crates, slumping to the floor, blood gushing from his wound and fell still. No memories, no impressions flew between this time, as if the man had died too quickly.

Never found his knees, flicking his wrist to break the flow.

Harstas stood, face drained of colour, bow faltering. His nostrils flared as he trembled. Never pointed a bloody hand at him. "Stay back and I will let you live."

The Vadiya commander's jaw worked.

Never backed toward the aqueduct's entry. Harstas took a single step forward and Never let his blood surge a little; it strained for the still-pumping blood from the Steelhawk but Harstas didn't know that. The commander flinched.

At the hatch, Never stepped down to the first rung of a ladder.

"Do not follow me."

He took another step down, the image of Harstas glaring after him the last thing he saw before darkness cloaked him.

~~

Time had passed – as it tended to do. How much, he couldn't know. At times he had to stop and hold the wall to keep the tunnel from swimming, a disconcerting experience in the darkness.

But Harstas had not followed.

Was it fear that kept the man at bay? Never shivered as he splashed along in the darkness. There was still a chance the commander would find him. If he watched the waterways...

Never winced when he stumbled. Dried blood pulled at the wound on his back where his clothing stuck to the skin. Blood still seeped from his thigh and arm, slowly at least. The slice on the back of his hand had already healed – his curse had a strange sense of humour in that way. Or was it cruelty?

A column of light appeared ahead.

He slowed when he reached it, blinking up at a ladder. Grating covered an opening. He climbed, grinding his teeth at the pain. Pushing the grate open, he hauled himself out into a domed room. Warm dawn light poured through glass in a window. The room was empty save for cleaning implements.

When he tried the door it opened to a quiet backstreet

near the wall.

Beyond the palace grounds.

Pacela's Spire cast a long shadow where it shone high above, still distant. Smoke streaked the lightening sky too. Dragging his feet forward, Never reached a corner and leant against a statue of Pacela, his shoulder resting on her slender hips. "Sorry Lady," he gasped out between breaths.

Smoke still pumped from parts of the palace.

Just how many Vadiya were in there?

Never glanced around empty streets. Empty streets. Was everyone hiding? It was dawn, yet in a city like Isacina, someone was always awake, always working. His mind circled to the logical conclusion – invasion.

The Vadiya had invaded – Gods, why?

It did not matter for now. He had a map that unlocked the secrets of the Amber Isle, a new clue to follow. Maybe it wasn't much but an odd sense of familiarity was undeniable when he'd looked it over. And after exhausting so many clues he had no choice but to take a risk. Men had died for the map; he had to try it. Never stumbled on, heading down toward Ashina's Oaks. Or, if he couldn't make it that far, the Water Petal.

His strength flagged before he found the Water Petal but a familiar tailor's shop appeared at the end of the street. Its sign beckoned to him, a giant, golden needle gleaming in the morning light. By the time he reached it the wound in his back had reopened and his vision was blurring again. He leant against the wall, labouring for air.

A door opened nearby, followed by a gasp and a slam.

"Thanks for the help," he murmured.

The Water Petal was a mere half-dozen steps across the

street yet he couldn't take the first one. His body ached, the wound on his back throbbed along with his arm and leg and worse, his vision continued to grow less and less reliable.

After all – why would a multi-coloured child be approaching him, eyes wide enough to swallow his face, drawing a wobbling horse after?

"Never?"

It spoke!

"Never, it's me – Temilo."

He frowned. Familiar. "The puppet-boy?"

"Yes, the jester. What happened?"

He breathed deeply and his vision began to clear. Temilo's face was full of concern. "The Vadiya attacked the palace," Never said.

"They attacked the whole city. Vento says I should flee... but I want to stay."

"You're working here?"

"Yes," he said with a small smile. "As a stable hand for now."

A shout echoed up the street – Vadiya words. Never twisted. Steelhawks and regular infantry, pointing and demanding he halt. Friends of Harstas?

"You, boy. Stand away from that man," came the order in accented Marlosi.

They knew.

His heart dragged in his chest; he had no more strength to run. He drew a knife, perhaps he could take at least one of them down.

"Here." Temilo pressed something into his free hand. Leather – reins. "Flee!"

"You should go, lad."

"No. You protected me before, at the gates. I owe you a life-debt."

"They'll kill you for helping me."

"Only if they catch me," Temilo said, and ran for the inn, shedding pieces of coloured clothing as he did. Never took half a step after him but it was too late, the Vadiya had started forward, shouting and waving weapons.

No bows at least.

Still Never hesitated. Would Temilo escape?

The thunder of boots neared. Never swore as he gripped the horse, stepping into the stirrup to fling his other leg over the saddle with the vilest curse he could think of – then he snapped the reins and his mount took off, thumping down the street.

He glanced back once and the Vadiya were receding.

If he could hold onto the horse he might just escape. As he clattered down the cobblestones he ground his teeth. There, the great trees lay ahead now, green canopies towering over the buildings. No Vadiya in sight. Somehow he held onto the horse, despite the pain, and charged through the empty gates, stirring leaves as he did.

Escape.

He didn't slow until he found himself crossing the plains, where he passed evidence of people who'd already fled the city: discarded pieces of clothing or cooking items, a single shoe, a trampled doll. He finally reined the horse in to rest; it breathed hard and he patted its neck.

He turned back to the city and growled.

Silvery lines of soldiers poured down from the mountains, streaming into the palace like shining serpents. War had come and Marlosa had been caught sleeping. For the people of Isacina, woe and misery was upon them.

Never swore again. Futile words.

Even if he bore no wounds there was nothing he could do. He turned his mount from the seat of the Empire and north toward the coast and the Grey Chain. At its end waited the Amber Isle, weeks away yet but a tiny glimmer of hope nonetheless.

Never took one more look at the city.

A glimpse of the sun flashing off armour near the gates – Harstas and his men, no doubt.

"Fine, Harstas. Follow me if you can."

Thanks for reading!

If you enjoyed *The Yellow Butterfly,* you might enjoy another story set in Japan, *A Whisper of Leaves.* Here's the blurb:

*When ESL teacher Riko finds an old journal buried in the forests beneath Mt Fuji, a malevolent, untraceable force begins to threaten her at every turn.*

*But is it all in her head?*

*The more she studies the journal for answers, the more questions she uncovers. Worse, no-one takes her fears seriously and her best lead appears to be a belligerent old man, whose only care in the world is raking leaves deep in the forest.*

*With her grip on reality shaken and friendships strained to breaking point, Riko has to discover the truth about the journal in order to put ghosts of the past to rest, as strange events turn deadly.*

If you enjoyed *Esmeralda*, you might like to see more from Thomas and Mia in *The Red Hourglass*. Here's the blurb:

*Escape isn't the hardest challenge for a slave – it's staying free afterwards.*

*Siblings Thomas and Mia find themselves fleeing across a desolate land, hounded by the monstrous sand-hog, a steam-powered war machine bent on recapturing them at all costs.*

*Thomas fears the worst. He knows the tyrannical King Williams seeks Mia and her mysterious powers of foresight, but it seems even her gift cannot save the day when the sand-hog corners them. It isn't until they cross paths with a group of rebels and stumble across rumours of a lost airship that Thomas begins to wonder if there isn't hope of escape after all...*

*A steampunk adventure set in a slowly dying land where magic clashes with steam and alchemy.*

Or if you liked the mild horror of *Dust*, you might also enjoy *Crossings*. Here's the blurb:

*Deep in the Australian bush, something dark is stirring.*

*When wildlife ranger Lisa Thomas finds a pile of animal entrails on her doorstep she immediately suspects her abusive ex, but the sudden spate of deaths that follow seem beyond even Ben's vindictiveness.*

*Worse, her father's health is deteriorating fast and when the harassment and deaths continue, it only fuels her feelings of powerlessness. To add confusion to growing fear, Lisa must also investigate reports of a giant white kangaroo, reports that suggest the creature is no mere hoax.*

*Yet the mysterious kangaroo is impossible to track down and the more Lisa searches the more she's sure an even greater threat lurks in the wilderness...*

If you enjoyed the contemporary fantasy of *Somnus and the March Hare*, you might like *The Fairy Wren* just as much. Here's the blurb:

*From the moment a fairy wren drops his lost wedding ring at his feet, Paul realises there's more magic to the world than he thought...*

*When Paul Fischer receives a strange phone call asking for help, from a woman who might be his estranged wife Rachel, he's drawn into a mysterious search that threatens not only his struggling bookstore, but long-buried dreams too.*

*Unfortunately, the only help comes from a shady best friend, an Italian run away and a strange blue fairy wren that seems to be trying to tell him something –yet the further he follows the clues it leaves the less sense the world seems to make. Is he on the verge of a magical, beautiful discovery or at the point of total disaster?*

If you enjoyed *The Hills of Tanakwi,* you might like the epic fantasy *City of Masks.* Here's the blurb:

*Waking in Anaskar Prison, covered in blood and accused of murder, nobody will listen to Notch's claims of innocence until he meets the future Protector of the Monarchy, Sofia Falco.*

*But Sofia has her own burdens. The first female Protector in a hundred years, her House is under threat from enemies within, the prince has made it clear he does not want her services and worst of all, she cannot communicate with her father's sentient mask of bone, the centuries-old Argeon. Without the bone mask she cannot help anyone -- not herself, and certainly not a mercenary with no powerful House to protect him.*

*Meanwhile, far across the western desert, Ain, a young Pathfinder, is thrust into the role of Seeker. Before winter storms close the way, he must leave his home on a quest to locate the Sea Shrine and take revenge on the people who drove his ancestors from Anaskar, the city ruled by the prince Sofia and Notch are sworn to protect, whether he wants their help or not.*

If you enjoyed the *Never (Prequel)*, you might like the epic fantasy sequel *The Amber Isle*. Here's the blurb:

*After years of running down dead-end clues, the rogue Never has nearly given up his quest for answers; his blood is cursed and his true name a mystery, yet no library, no healer and none who claim to know dark magics have ever been able to help.*

*Until he steals a map to the mysterious Amber Isle, which might just hold the answers he needs.*

*But Never isn't the only one who wants the map – an old enemy, Commander Harstas, also seeks it and Harstas craves revenge for the deaths of his men.*

*Forced to flee through a war zone, Never soon stumbles across a group of treasure-hunters hoping to discover the wonders of the Amber Isle for themselves. But the deeper they venture into the Isle, the more deadly it grows.*

*Trapped between the greed of the treasure hunters, cunning traps in the Isle itself, the threat of Harstas' fury and his own desperation to finally uncover answers, Never must find a way to unlock the Isle's ancient secrets and escape – or perish without ever learning the truth.*

## Acknowledgements

For this collection I wanted to bring together various short stories that I'd written over the last five years or so but also (hopefully) to introduce people to some of my other works of fiction, so I hope you found something you enjoyed here!

A lot of folks helped me with these stories at different times over the years, certainly my editor Amanda, but also Tracy, Ambrose and the Alchemists too. Also, the teams behind the Steampunk Fairy Tale collections, the Horror Fairy Tale collection, Spark: A journal of New Writing and Medium, where some of the stories within this collection were previously published.

I'd also like to thank David and also Rebekah for their hard work on this collection too.

Thanks for reading!

Ashley